MSU LIBRARIES
3 2109 00096 3240

D1520971

GLOSSARY OF THE THEATRE

GLOSSARIA INTERPRETUM

Published by

AUSLANDS- UND DOLMETSCHERINSTITUT DER
JOHANNES GUTENBERG-UNIVERSITÄT
MAINZ IN GERMERSHEIM
DOLMETSCHER-INSTITUT DER UNIVERSITÄT HEIDELBERG
ÉCOLE D'INTERPRÈTES DE L'UNIVERSITÉ DE GENÈVE
ÉCOLE SUPÉRIEURE D'INTERPRÈTES ET DE
TRADUCTEURS DE L'UNIVERSITÉ DE PARIS
INSTITUTE OF LANGUAGES AND LINGUISTICS
GEORGETOWN UNIVERSITY, WASHINGTON, D.C.
SCUOLA DI LINGUE MODERNE PER TRADUTTORI
ED INTERPRETI DI CONFERENZE, UNIVERSITÀ
DEGLI STUDI DI TRIESTE

under the General Editorship of

PROF. JEAN HERBERT
FORMER CHIEF INTERPRETER TO THE UNITED NATIONS

ELSEVIER PUBLISHING COMPANY
AMSTERDAM / LONDON / NEW YORK
1969

GLOSSARY OF THE THEATRE

IN

ENGLISH, FRENCH, ITALIAN AND GERMAN

COMPILED AND ARRANGED BY

KARIN R. M. BAND-KUZMANY,
DIPL. DOLM. VIENNA

ELSEVIER PUBLISHING COMPANY
AMSTERDAM / LONDON / NEW YORK
1969

ELSEVIER PUBLISHING COMPANY
335 JAN VAN GALENSTRAAT, P.O. BOX 211, AMSTERDAM

AMERICAN ELSEVIER PUBLISHING COMPANY, INC.
52 VANDERBILT AVENUE, NEW YORK, N.Y. 10017

ELSEVIER PUBLISHING COMPANY LIMITED
RIPPLESIDE COMMERCIAL ESTATE
BARKING, ESSEX

Library of Congress Card Number: 68-57152

Standard Book Number: 444-40716-2

Printed in The Netherlands

FOREWORD

Iow that conferences deal with such a multitude of questions and the attainments equired of their interpreters have grown so diverse and specialized, we feel that nere is room for a series of multilingual technical glossaries bearing on the rincipal subjects discussed at international conferences.

This undertaking is being supervised and co-ordinated by M. Jean Herbert, ormerly Chief Interpreter to the United Nations. The purpose of its joint ponsorship by the Auslands- und Dolmetscherinstitut der Johannes Gutenberg-niversität Mainz in Germersheim, the Dolmetscherinstitut der Universität leidelberg, the École d'Interprètes de l'Université de Genève, the École upérieure d'Interprètes et de Traducteurs de l'Université de Paris, the Institute of anguages and Linguistics, Georgetown University, Washington, D.C., and the cuola di Lingue moderne per Traduttori ed Interpreti di Conferenze, Università egli Studi di Trieste, is to emphasize the international and scientific character of nese glossaries. They are the work of language experts, including interpreters, ome of whom are teachers or alumni of the sponsoring institutes.

The aim of these glossaries is to endow professional and apprentice nterpreters with a terminological apparatus both scientifically planned and enerally acknowledged in the various sectors of international activity. In broader rms, their intention is to enable experts to understand one another more readily, nd to disseminate an accepted international terminology.

Each glossary will appear in several languages, to be chosen according to the equency of their use at international conferences on that particular subject.

We have set out to make the glossaries as compact and efficient as possible. he usual order of terms is alphabetical, although a certain number are specially sted by their functions.

It is hoped that several glossaries will appear annually, dealing successively ith subjects likely to arise at conferences where trained interpreters are employed.

R. B. BEINERT, Direktor des Dolmetscherinstituts der Universität Heidelberg

ROF. DR. R. BRUMMER, Direktor des Auslands- und Dolmetscherinstituts der Johannes Gutenberg-Universität Mainz in Germersheim

ROF. CLAUDIO CALZOLARI, Preside della Facoltà di Economia e Commercio, Direttore della Scuola di Lingue moderne per Traduttori ed Interpreti di Conferenze dell'Università degli Studi di Trieste

AURICE GRAVIER, Directeur de l'École supérieure d'Interprètes et de Traducteurs de l'Université de Paris

TEFAN F. HORN, Head, Division of Interpretation and Translation, Institute of Languages and Linguistics, Georgetown University, Washington, D.C.

STELLING-MICHAUD, Professeur à la Faculté des Lettres, Administrateur de l'École d'Interprètes de l'Université de Genève

TITLES PUBLISHED IN THE SERIES GLOSSARIA INTERPRETUM

G1 CONFERENCE TERMINOLOGY-Jean Herbert (second editor), 756 entrie in English, French, Spanish, Russian, Italian, German, 174 pages, 196 Arabic - English - French edition also available.

G2 NUCLEAR PHYSICS AND ATOMIC ENERGY-G.J. Béné, 2117 entries i English, French, German, Russian, 222 pages, 1960

G3 CHEMINS DE FER-Bureau International de Documentation des Chemin de Fer, 1995 entries in French, German, English, Italian, Spanis Swedish, 422 pages, 1960

G4 PROVERBES FRANÇAIS-Gérard Ilg, 607 entries in French with tran lations in English, German, Dutch, Italian, Spanish, Latin, 110 page 1960

G5 DETERGENTS-G. Carrière, 257 entries in 19 languages, 149 pages, 1960

G6 QUAESTIONARIUM MEDICUM-F. Meyboom, 457 phrases in 17 language 222 pages, 1961

G7 INTERNAL COMBUSTION ENGINE-Shell International Petroleum Co pany Ltd., 1164 entries in English, French, German, Italian, Dutc Spanish, Portuguese, Russian, 286 pages, 1961

G8 OBSTÉTRIQUE ET GYNÉCOLOGIE-N.C. Louros, 2576 entries in Frenc Latin, English, Russian, German, Spanish, Italian, Greek, 452 page 1964

G9 HEMATOLOGY-L. Romei-Braconi, 2210 entries in English, Frenc Spanish, Italian, German, Russian, 314 pages, 1964

G10 GLOSSARY OF FINANCIAL TERMS-Stefan F. Horn, 2278 entries English, French, Spanish, German, 280 pages, 1965

G11 GLOSSARY OF ECONOMICS including Soviet Terminology-F. and Clifford Vaughan, 1669 entries in English, French, German, Russia 210 pages, 1966

G12 GLOSSARY OF GEOGRAPHICAL NAMES-G. Lana, L. Iasbez, L. Mea 5950 names in English, French, Spanish, Italian, Dutch, Germa 192 pages, 1967

G13 SUGAR-BEET GLOSSARY-Institut International de Recherches Bet ravières, 1500 entries in English, French, German, Latin, 178 pag 1967

G15 GLOSSARY OF THE THEATRE-K. Band-Kuzmany, 1115 entries English, French, Italian, German, 130 pages, 1969

IN PREPARATION:

G14 GLOSSARY OF INTERNATIONAL TREATIES - Y. Renoux, J. Ya 1088 entries in French, English, Italian, Spanish, Dutch, Germ Russian, approx. 250 pages, 1970

G16 GLOSSARY OF GENETICS - F. Biass-Ducroux, approx. 2950 entries English, French, Italian, Spanish, German, Russian, 1970

PREFACE

Le théâtre est lieu de rencontre, la communauté s'y regroupe, les personnages fictifs y affrontent de simples humains qui, pour ce rendez-vous, s'arrachent aux routines de la vie quotidienne, l'auteur y jette ses idées en pâture au public. La légende reprend vie, le passé ressurgit devant le présent. La farce succède à la tragédie. Le réalisme s'allie bien souvent au lyrisme. Le choeur des Muses se reforme sur la scène, poésie, musique, danse s'associent dans le drame lyrique ou l'opéra. Le théâtre exige aussi, dans sa pratique, non plus la rencontre provisoire mais l'alliance et la coopération intimes de multiples techniques: techniques humaines d'abord, celles de l'acteur, du musicien, du danseur, mimique, diction, chorégraphie, maîtrise corporelle et psychologique prise sous ses aspects les plus divers. Techniques artistiques, celles de la plastique, art du décorateur et de l'éclairagiste, du costumier et de l'accessoiriste, maîtrise de l'accoustique, formation du chanteur soliste, des choeurs et de l'orchestre, raffinement de la sonorisation. Règnant sur l'ensemble de ces activités, moins visible que le chef d'orchestre au concert mais non moins efficace, le maître d'oeuvre, intermédiaire indispensable (mais parfois indiscret) entre l'auteur et le public. N'oublions pas l'édifice lui-même. Le théâtre suppose le lieu théâtral, l'art du scénographe, de l'architecte semble premier, préalable à tous les autres, une nouvelle conception de la scène, de l'aire de jeu risque d'entraîner une mutation dans les rapports entre les comédiens et le public, elle peut même influencer l'écriture des auteurs dramatiques. C'est aussi l'architecte qui installe et abrite le public, lui donne ses aises pendant qu'il assiste à la cérémonie théâtrale mais qui doit encore lui permettre d'entrer facilement dans la salle et lui ouvre l'accès de foyers vastes et attrayants, quand vient l'heure de l'entr'acte.

Dans ces conditions, on le comprendra facilement, il n'est pas aisé de délimiter un "vocabulaire du théâtre". Quand on se tourne vers des techniques modernes de l'industrie ou de la recherche scientifique, on arrive plus facilement à tracer les limites d'un vocabulaire spécifique. Le théâtre appartient à la plus lointaine histoire et s'empare au fur et à mesure de toutes les innovations que peut lui fournir la science moderne. Il tient de l'art, de la littérature et de la technologie la plus poussée. Il revêt des aspects commerciaux et il intéresse le sociologue comme aussi l'historien des idées. Enfin le théâtre ne reconnaît pas les frontières politiques ni même les frontières linguistiques. Une pièce qui connaît un grand succès à Londres, à New York, à Stockholm ou à Paris a toutes chances d'être traduite dans une dizaine de langues, adaptée et parfois profondément transformée (ou trahie) et de connaître des fortunes diverses un peu partout dans le monde. Les troupes partent en tournée et circulent loin de leur pays d'origine, parfois avec un équipement léger, souvent accompagnées d'un matériel lourd et d'un groupe de techniciens et de machinistes.

Il fallait donc absolument consacrer un glossaire à l'art théâtral et aux activités qui s'y rattachent. D'excellents spécialistes se sont appliqués à résoudre les multiples problèmes qui soulève l'élaboration de cet important recueil. Ils ne se sont pas laissé arrêter par l'étendue du domaine à couvrir. Il faut les en remercier, ils ont utilement oeuvré pour que vive le théâtre!

Maurice GRAVIER
Professeur à la Sorbonne
Directeur de l'École Supérieure d'Interprètes
et de Traducteurs de l'Université de Paris

LANGUAGE INDICATIONS

d	Deutsch
f	français
i	Italiano

ABBREVIATIONS

adj.	adjective
adv.	adverb
coll.	colloquial
hist.	historical
sl.	slang

(GB)	term especially used in Great Britain
(US)	term mainly used in North America

ACKNOWLEDGEMENT

The author would like to express her thanks to Mr. Richard Southern, who very kindly checked the English part of the manuscript several years ago, as well as to the Universities of Paris and Trieste, for their assistance in the compilation of the French and Italian sections.

BASIC TABLE

1 ABDOMINAL BREATHING
f respiration abdominale
i respirazione addominale
d Bauchatmung

2 ABRIDGED VERSION;
CUT VERSION
f version abrégée
i versione ridotta
d gekürzte Fassung

3 ABSTRACT STYLE
f style abstrait
i stile astratto
d abstrakter Stil

4 ACCESSORIES
f accessoires
i accessori
d Zubehör

5 ACOUSTIC INSTALLATION
f installation sonore
i impianto sonoro
d akustische Einrichtung

6 ACOUSTICS
f acoustique
i acustica
d Akustik

7 ACROBAT
f acrobate
i acrobata
d Akrobat

8 ACT, to;
to PERFORM;
to PLAY
f jouer
i recitare
d darstellen; spielen

9 ACT
f acte
i atto
d Akt; Aufzug

10 ACTABLE
f efficace; jouable
i recitabile; che si può recitare; che si presta ad essere recitato
d spielbar; bühnenwirksam

11 ACT DROP
f rideau de manoeuvre
i calare del sipario, il
d Aktvorhang; Zwischenakts-vorhang

12 ACTING;
PRESENTATION;
PORTRAYING
f le jeu; la représentation
i recitare, il; recita; recitazione
d Darstellung

13 ACTING AREA;
PLAYING AREA
f espace scénique
i campo di azione
d Spielraum

14 ACTING EDITION;
STAGE VERSION;
ACTING VERSION
f version scénique
i versione per la scena
d Bühnenfassung

15 ACTING GROUP;
DRAMATIC SOCIETY;
COMPANY;
ENSEMBLE
f compagnie; troupe fixe
i compagnia
d Ensemble; Schauspieler-gesellschaft

16 ACTING PLANE
f aire de jeu
i campo di azione
d Spielfläche

17 ACTING STYLE
f style de jeu
i stile nel recitare
d schauspielerischer Stil

ACTING VERSION see 14 ACTING EDITION

18 ACTION;
STORY;
PLOT
f intrigue; action
i azione; intreccio
d Handlung

19 ACTOR
f acteur; comédien; cabotin
i attore
d Schauspieler; Komödiant

20 ACTOR-LIKE;
HISTRIONIC
f théâtral; cabotin
i teatrale; istrionico
d schauspielerisch

21 ACTOR-MANAGER
f acteur-chef de troupe
i capocomico
d Schauspieler-Direktor

22 ACTORS' EQUITY
f syndicat des acteurs
i associazione degli artisti; sindacato degli artisti
d Bühnengewerkschaft

23 ACTORS' THEATRE
f théâtre d'acteurs
i Teatro di Attori
d Schauspielertheater

24 ACTRESS
f comédienne; actrice
i attrice
d Schauspielerin

25 ACT WAIT;
PAUSE;
INTERVAL;
INTERMISSION
f entr'acte
i intervallo
d Pause

26 ACT WARNING
f signal de début d'acte; signal d'entrée en scène
i segnale dell'inizio dell'atto
d Richtzeichen

27 ADAPT, to
to CONVERT (a building)
f adapter; transformer (un théâtre)
i adattare; trasformare
d adaptieren

28 ADAPTATION
f adaptation scénique
i adattamento scenico
d Bühnenbearbeitung

29 AD-LIB, to;
to IMPROVISE
f improviser
i improvvisare
d extemporieren

30 ADMINISTRATOR
f Directeur général d'un théâtre subventionné
i amministratore
d Generalintendant

31 ADVANCE BOOKING
f location
i prenotazione
d Vorverkauf; Kartenvorverkauf

32 AGENT'S OFFICE;
BOOKING AGENCY
f bureau de location; agence de location
i agenzia di prenotazione
d Agentur; Kartenbüro

33 ALFRESCO PERFORMANCE;
OUT-OF-DOOR PERFORMANCE;
OPEN-AIR PERFORMANCE
f représentation de plein air
i rappresentazione all'aperto; recita all aperto
d Freilichtaufführung

34 ALIENATION EFFECT
f effet "V"; effet d'éloignement
i effetto V
d Verfremdungseffekt

35 ALLEGORY
f allégorie
i allegoria
d Allegorie

36 ALL OFF, PLEASE!
f en coulisses!
i tutti fuori!
d Von der Bühne!

37 ALLUSION
f allusion
i allusione
d Anspielung

38 ALTERNATE PARTS, to
f alterner les rôles
i alternare le parti
d alternieren

39 AMATEUR
f amateur
i amatore
d Amateur

40 AMATEUR THEATRE
f théâtre amateur
i teatro di dilettanti
d Amateurtheater; Liebhabertheater; Laienbühne

41 AMATEUR THEATRICALS; PLAY FOR AMATEURS
f pièce pour amateurs
i recita per dilettanti
d Laienspiel

42 AMPHITHEATRE
f amphithéâtre
i anfiteatro
d Amphitheater

43 ANALYTICAL PLAYWRITING
f technique analytique
i tecnica analitica
d analytische Technik

44 ANGEL (coll.); SPONSOR; BACKER
f commanditaire
i finanziatore teatrale
d Geldgeber

45 ANGULAR MOVEMENTS
f mouvements gauches
i movimenti bruschi
d eckige Bewegungen

46 ANNOUNCE, to; to INTRODUCE; to EMCEE (US)
f annoncer; introduire
i annunciare
d ansagen

47 ANTAGONIST
f antagoniste
i antagonista
d Gegenspieler; Antagonist

48 ANTICHRIST PLAY
f jeu de l'antéchrist
i recita del anticristo
d Antichristspiel

49 ANTICS
f bouffonneries; farces
i buffoneria; farsa
d Possen

50 ANTISTROPHE
f antistrophe
i antistrofe
d Gegenstrophe

51 APOTHEOSIS
f apothéose
i apoteosi
d Apotheose

52 APPEAR, to; to MAKE AN ENTRANCE; to COME ON; to ENTER
f entrer; apparaitre; faire son entrée
i entrare; presentarsi
d auftreten

53 APPEARANCE;
ENTRANCE
f entrée; apparition
i entrata; apparizione
d Auftritt

54 APPLAUSE;
HAND;
ROUND
f applaudissement
i applauso
d Applaus; Beifall

55 APPLAUSE DURING THE ACTION
f applaudissements pendant le jeu
i applausi durante la recita; applausi a scena aperta
d Szenenapplaus

56 APPLY MAKE-UP, to
f étendre (fard); appliquer (fard)
i truccare
d auftragen (Schminke)

57 APPRENTICESHIP
f apprentissage
i apprendistato
d Lehrzeit

58 APRON STAGE
f proscénium
i proscenio
d Vorderbühne

59 ARCH;
ARCHWAY;
CUT CLOTH
f principale
i arcata centrale; architrave
d Bogen

60 AREA LIGHTING
f éclairage général; éclairage diffus
i zona d'illuminazione
d Flächenbeleuchtung

61 ARENA STAGE;
THEATRE-IN-THE-ROUND;
CIRCUS STAGE
f arène; théâtre en rond
i teatro a scena circolare; arena
d Arenabühne

62 ART DRAMA
f pièce artistique; théâtre d'art
i dramma intellettuale
d Kunstdrama

63 ARTICULATION;
ENUNCIATION
f articulation
i articolazione
d Artikulation

64 ARTIFICIAL
f artificiel
i artificiale
d gekünstelt

65 ARTIST;
ARTISTE
f artiste
i artista
d Künstler; Künstlerin

66 ARTISTS' ENTRANCE
f entrée des artistes
i entrata degli artisti
d Künstlereingang

67 ART THEATRE
f Théâtre d'Art
i Teatro d'Arte
d Künstlerisches Theater

68 ASBESTOS CURTAIN;
SAFETY CURTAIN
f rideau de fer; rideau de sécurité
i sipario di sicurezza
d eiserner Vorhang

69 ASIDE
f aparté
i a parte
d Aparte

70 ASSISTANT DIRECTOR;
ASSISTANT PRODUCER;
ASSISTANT STAGE MANAGER (ASM)
f assistant metteur en scène; assistant à la mise en scène
i aiuto regista; assistente regista
d Regieassistent; Hilfsregisseur

71 ASSISTANT ELECTRICIAN
f aide électricien
i aiuto elettricista
d Hilfsbeleuchter

ASSISTANT PRODUCER see 70 ASSISTANT DIRECTOR

72 ASSISTANT STAGE MANAGER;
SOUSRÉGISSEUR
f sans equiv. (metteur en scène chargé d'assister à la représentation)
i aiuto del direttore tecnico delle scene
d Abendregisseur

ASSISTANT STAGE MANAGER (ASM) see 70 ASSISTANT DIRECTOR

73 ATELLAN FARCES
f atellanes
i atellane
d Atellanenspiele

74 ATTITUDE
f attitude; pose
i attitudine; posa
d Attitüde

75 ATTRACTION;
BOX-OFFICE APPEAL;
DRAWING POWER
f force d'attraction
i attrazione
d Zugkraft

76 AUDIENCE
f public
i pubblico
d Publikum; Zuschauer

77 AUDIENCE-DIRECTED
f (adressé) au public
i rivolto al pubblico
d publikumsgerichtet

78 AUDIENCE'S LEFT
f côté jardin
i a destra del palcoscenico
d links vom Zuschauer

79 AUDIENCE'S RIGHT
f côté cour
i a sinistra del palcoscenico
d rechts vom Zuschauer

80 AUDITION
f audition
i audizione
d Vorsprechen

81 AUDITORIUM;
HALL;
HOUSE
f salle
i sala; auditorio
d Saal; Zuschauerraum

82 AUTOGRAPH
f autographe
i autografo
d Autogramm

83 AUTOGRAPH HOUND;
AUTOGRAPH HUNTER
f chasseur d'autographes
i cacciatore di autografi
d Autogrammjäger

84 AVANT-GARDE
f avant-garde
i avanguardia
d Avantgarde

85 BABY SPOT
f spot
i piccolo proiettore
d Kleinscheinwerfer

86 BACK CLOTH
f toile de fond
i sfondo; fondale
d Hinterhänger; Prospekt

87 BACK-CLOTH;
BACKDROP;
BACKGROUND
f lointain; arrière-plan
i sfondo
d Hintergrund

BACKER see 44 ANGEL

BACKGROUND see 87 BACK-CLOTH

88 BACKGROUND NOISES
f bruitage; bruits de coulisse
i dietro alle quinte; voci di corridoio
d Geräuschkulisse

89 BACKING
f pantalon
i fondino
d Hintersetzer

90 BACKSTAGE
f l'arrière-scène
i camerino; zona dietro la scena
d Hinterbühne

91 BACKSTAGE (adv.);
BEHIND-SCENES
f dans les coulisses
i dietro la scena
d hinter den Kulissen; hinter der Szene

92 BACKSTAGE INFLUENCE
f protection; "Piston"
i raccomandazione
d Protektion

93 BACK WALL
f mur du fond; lointain
i muro di fondo
d Bühnenruckwand

94 BAD JOIN;
CRACK;
GAP
f rayon lumineux (parallèle à la rampe); fente de lumière
i fessura da cui esce la luce
d Lichtspalt

95 BALCONY
f balcon
i balconata
d Balkon

96 BALD WIG
f faux crâne
i parrucca
d Glatzenperücke

97 BALLAD, (DOGGEREL);
BROADSIDE BALLAD
f chanson populaire
i ballata popolare
d Bänkellied

98 BALLAD SINGER
f chanteur des rues
i menestrello cantinbanco
d Bänkelsänger

99 BALLOON, to;
to WING IT;
to STICK;
to DRY UP
f avoir un trou; avoir un blanc
i avere una amnesia; dimenticare la battuta
d hängen bleiben

100 BALUSTRADE
f balustrade
i balaustra
d Balustrade

101 BAND;
COMPANY;
TROUPE;
TROOP (US)
f troupe
i compagnia
d Bande; Truppe

102 BAR
f bar
i bar
d Buffet

103 BAR BELL;
INTERMISSION BELL
f sonnerie d'entr'acte
i campanello d'avviso
d Pausenglocke

104 BARNSTORMERS (coll.);
TOURING COMPANY;
STROLLING PLAYERS;
ITINERANT PLAYERS;
FIT-UP
f troupe ambulante
i compagnia di giro
d Wanderbühne; Wandertruppe

105 BAROQUE STAGE
f scène baroque
i scena barocca
d Barockbühne

106 BARREL;
PIPE BATTEN
f porteuse; perche
i sbarra delle centine
d Laststange

107 BASKET BOX;
LATTICE BOX;
LETTICE BOX
f loge secrète; loge dissimulée
i palco graticolato
d Incognitologe

108 BATTEN
f battant
i cantinella
d Latte

109 BATTENED-OUT
f charpenté; armé de battants
i costruito con cantinelle
d ausgesteift

110 BATTENED-OUT CLOTH
f toile; décor sur châssis; châssis
i tela su quinta
d ausgesteifte Dekoration

111 BEGIN!
f allez-y!; commencez!
i si inizia!; si incomincia!; si va sù! (sl.)
d Los; anfangen!

BEHIND-SCENES see 91 BACKSTAGE

112 BENEFIT NIGHT;
BENEFIT PERFORMANCE
f gala de bienfaisance
i serata di beneficenza; spettacolo di beneficenza
d Benefizvorstellung

113 BEST PART (an actor's)
f rôle en or; meilleur rôle
i il ruolo migliore; la migliore interpretazione
d Paraderolle

114 BIOMECHANICAL STYLE;
BIOMECHANICS
f style biomécanique
i biomeccanica
d Biomechanik

115 BIS;
ENCORE
f bis; da capo

i bis!
d da capo

116 BIT (part);
TWO LINES AND A SPIT (sl.);
SMALL PART
f petit rôle
i piccola parte
d Röllchen

117 BLACK-AND-WHITE PORTRAITURE;
SOOT-AND-WHITEWASH CHARACTERIZATION
f composition contrastée à l'excès
i personnaggio contrastato; caratterizzazione contrastata
d Schwarzweiss-Zeichnung

118 BLACKOUT
f faire le noir
i oscuramento
d Blackout

119 BLANK VERSE
f vers blanc
i verso sciolto
d Blankvers

120 BLIND BOOKING
f louer (une place) sans connaitre le spectacle; louer (une place) à l'aveuglette
i prenotare senza conoscere lo spettacolo
d blindbuchen

121 BLUE-PENCIL, to;
to CUT;
to DELETE
f couper
i sopprimere; togliere; censurare
d streichen

122 BLUE-PENCILLING;
CUTTING
f coupure
i il sopprimere una parte
d Kürzung

123 BOARDS, the
f les planches
i il palcoscenico
d Bretter, die die Welt bedeuten

124 BOAT TRUCK;
WAGON
f chariot; plateforme coulissante; plateau mobile
i palcoscenico scorrevole per il rapido cambiamento di scena
d Bühnenwagen

125 BOMBAST;
FUSTIAN
f emphase; grandiloquence
i magniloquenza; ampollosità; emfasi
d Bombast; falsches Pathos; Schwulst

126 BOOK
f brochure
i opuscolo
d Rollenheft

127 BOOK CEILING
f plafond à charnière
i soffitto a libro
d Klapp-Plafond

128 BOOK-FLAT
f châssis pliant
i fondale a paravento
d geklappte Wand

BOOKING AGENCY see 32 AGENT'S OFFICE

129 BOOTH STAGE;
SCAFFOLD STAGE
f trétaux (de foire)
i saltimbanchi di fiera; teatro di saltimbanchi
d Bretterbühne; Bude; Pawlatschen

130 BORDER
f frise
i soffitto
d Front; Soffitte

131 BOTTOM BATTEN
f latte inférieure
i pertica inferiore
d Unterlatte

132 BOULEVARD COMEDY; LIGHT FARCE
f comédie de boulevard
i commedia leggera
d Boulevardkomödie

133 BOURGEOIS COMEDY; DOMESTIC COMEDY
f comédie bourgeoise
i commedia borghese
d bürgerliches Schauspiel

134 BOX
f loge
i palco
d Loge

135 BOX FOR SPECIAL OCCASIONS
f loge d'honneur
i palco d'onore
d Festloge

136 BOX KEEPER
f ouvreuse
i maschera
d Logenschliesser

137 BOX OFFICE
f caisse
i biglietteria
d Kasse

BOX-OFFICE APPEAL see 75 ATTRACTION

138 BOX-OFFICE HIT; BOX-OFFICE SUCCESS
f succès commercial
i successo commerciale
d Kassenerfolg

139 BOX-OFFICE RECEIPTS; TAKINGS
f recette
i incassi
d Einnahmen

140 BOX SET
f décor fermé
i scena di camera
d geschlossenes Bühnenzimmer

141 BRACE, to
f entretoiser
i rafforzare con traverse
d verspreizen

142 BRACE
f béquille; écharpe
i sostegno
d Steife

143 BRAVURA PART
f morceau de bravoure
i parte di bravura
d Bravourstück

144 BREATH CONTROL; BREATHING TECHNIQUE
f technique respiratoire
i tecnica respiratoria
d Atemtechnik

145 BREATHING EXERCISES
f exercices respiratoires
i esercizi respiratori
d Atemübungen

146 BREECHES PART
f travesti
i travestimento
d Hosenrolle

147 BRIDGE
f trappe; plan mobile
i montacarichi sul palcoscenico
d Versenkung(stisch)

148 BRIDGE, (LIGHTING)
f pont; passerelle

i ponte praticabile
d Brücke

149 BROAD;
COARSE;
LOW
f vulgaire; gros
i volgare; grossolano
d derb

BROADSIDE BALLAD see 97 (DOGGEREL) BALLAD

150 BUFFOON;
JESTER;
MERRY ANDREW;
FUNNY MAN
f bouffon; plaisantin; farceur
i buffone; comico
d Possenreisser; Spassmacher

151 BUFFOONERY
f clownerie
i buffoneria
d Clownerie

152 "BUILD" A PART, to
f alléger
i creare un personnaggio
d auflockern

153 BUILD UP AN EXIT, to
f faire une bonne sortie
i creare le condizioni (per una buona uscita); preparare le condizioni (per una buona uscita)
d sich einen guten Abgang machen

154 BURLETTA;
BURLESQUE
f le burlesque
i burlesco
d Burleske

155 BUSINESS
f jeu de scène
i azione
d äussere Handlung

156 BUSKIN;
HIGH TRAGIC BOOT
f cothurne
i coturno
d Kothurn

157 BUTLER PART
f rôle de valet
i parte da servitone
d Dienerrolle

158 BUZZER;
CURTAIN WARNING SIGNAL
f sonnerie de rideau
i segnale elettrico di chiusura e apertura del sipario
d Aktzeichen

159 CABARET
f cabaret
i cabaret
d Kabarett

160 CABARET ARTIST
f artiste de cabaret
i artista di cabaret
d Kabarettist

161 CALL BOARD
f tableau de service
i indicatore di servizio
d schwarzes Brett

162 CALL BOY
f avertisseur
i buttafuori
d Inspizient (nearest equiv.)

163 CALL LIGHT
f signal d'entrée
i segnale luminoso di chiamata
d Auftrittszeichen

164 CALL LIST; SCHEDULE; TIME-TABLE
f tableau des répétitions; bulletin de service
i lista delle prove
d Probenplan

165 CAMPUS THEATRE (US); UNIVERSITY THEATRE
f théâtre universitaire
i teatro universitario
d Universitätstheater

166 CANCEL, to
f annuler
i annullare
d absagen

167 CANTEEN
f cantine
i mensa; dispensa
d Kantine

168 CANVAS, to
f entoiler
i intelaiare
d bespannen

169 CAPACITY (OF THE THEATER)
f capacité de la salle; nombre de places
i capacità (della sala); capienza (della sala)
d Platzanzahl

170 CAREER
f carrière
i carriera
d Karriere

171 CAR OF THESPIS
f chariot de Thespis
i carro di Tespi
d Thespiskarren

172 CARPET-CUT
f trapillon de tapis
i fissatore del tappeto
d Teppichschlitz

173 CAST, to
f distribuer (les rôles)
i distribuire le parti
d besetzen

174 CAST
f distribution
i elenco artistico
d Besetzung

175 CASTING
f distribution
i distribuzione
d Rollenbesetzung

176 CATHARSIS
f catharsis
i catarsi
d Katharsis

177 CELLAR THEATRE (Germany, Austria, etc)
- f cave; caveau
- i teatro di "cave"
- d Kellertheater

178 CENSOR
- f censeur
- i critico
- d Zensor

179 CENSORSHIP
- f censure
- i censura
- d Zensur

180 CENTRAL FIGURE; MAIN CHARACTER; CHIEF PERSON
- f personnage central; personnage principal
- i personaggio centrale; personaggio principale
- d Hauptgestalt; Zentralgestalt

181 CENTRE AISLE
- f allée centrale
- i corridoio centrale
- d Mittelgang

182 CHALK MARK
- f marque à la craie
- i segno fatto col gesso
- d Kreidezeichen

183 CHAMBER PLAY
- f pièce pour théâtre de chambre
- i commedia o tragedia per teatro da camera; rappresentazione da camera
- d Kammerspiel

184 CHAMBER THEATRE
- f théâtre de chambre
- i teatro da camera
- d Zimmertheater; Kammerspiele

185 CHANGE, to (scene); to RE-CONDITION (building)
- f changer de décor; remodeler
- i cambiare
- d umbauen

186 CHANGE OF PROGRAMME
- f changement de programme
- i cambiamento di programma
- d Programmwechsel; Spielplanänderung

187 CHANGE OF SCENE
- f changement de décor
- i cambiamento di scena
- d Umbau

188 CHARACTER-ACTOR
- f comédien qui joue les rôles de composition, les rôles chargés
- i caratterista
- d Chargendarsteller

189 CHARACTER CATEGORY; TYPE; CHARACTER TYPE
- f emploi; caractère
- i carattere stereotipato
- d Fach

190 CHARACTER COMEDIAN
- f rôle de caractère (comique)
- i comico che basa il suo umorismo sul carattere del personaggio che interpreta
- d Charakterkomiker

191 CHARACTER DRAWING; CHARACTER PORTRAYAL; CHARACTER DELINEATION
- f dessin du personnage
- i sviluppo artistico del personaggio
- d Charakterzeichnung

192 CHARACTERIZE, to
- f composer
- i caratterizzare; comporre
- d charakterisieren

193 CHARACTER MAN;
SPECIALIST
f comédien de caractère
i attore di carattere; primo attore; padre nobile; caratterista
d Charakterschauspieler; Chargendarsteller

194 CHARACTER PART
f rôle de caractère
i parte di carattere
d Charakterrolle

CHARACTER TYPE see 189 CHARACTER CATEGORY

195 CHARACTER WOMAN
f comédienne qui joue les rôles de composition; les rôles chargés
i caratterista
d Chargendarstellerin

196 CHARIVARI
f charivari
i serenata burlesca
d Charivari

197 CHARON'S STAIRCASE
f escalier de Charon
i scala di Caronte
d Charontische Stiege

198 CHEAP MUSIC-HALL
f music-hall à bon marché
i music-hall da strapazzo; music-hall di poco conto
d Tingeltangel

199 CHECK AT THE EXIT FOR APPLAUSE
f fausse sortie
i finta uscita
d falscher Abgang

200 CHECK ROOM (US);
WARDROBE (costumes);
DRESSING ROOM (actors');
COATROOM;
CLOAKROOM
f vestiaire (du public); loge (de l'acteur)
i guardaroba
d Garderobe

201 CHEMICAL STEAM
f vapeur chimique
i vapore chimico
d chemischer Dampf

202 CHEST BREATHING
f respiration pectorale
i respirazione pettorale
d Brustatmung

203 CHIEF ELECTRICIAN
f chef éclairagiste
i capo elettricista
d Beleuchtungsmeister

CHIEF PERSON see 180 CENTRAL FIGURE

204 CHILD PART
f rôle d'enfant
i parte da bambino
d Kinderrolle

205 CHILDREN'S PLAY
f pièce pour enfants
i recita per bambini; commedia per bambini
d Kinderstück

206 CHILDREN'S THEATRE
f théâtre pour enfants; théâtre d'enfants
i teatro per bambini
d Kindertheater

207 CHOIR;
CHORUS
f choeur
i coro
d Chor

208 CHOPPY
f haché
i stile rotto
d abgehackt

209 CHOREOGRAPHER
f chorégraphe
i coreografo
d Choreograph

210 CHOREOGRAPHY
f Chorégraphie
i coreografia
d Choreographie

CHORUS see 207 CHOIR

211 CHORUS DRESSING ROOM
f loge générale; loge des figurants
i camerino degli artisti; camerino delle comparse
d Sammelgarderobe; Statistengarderobe

212 CHORUS LEADER
f chef de choeur; choryphée
i direttore del coro
d Chorführer

213 CHRISTMAS PLAY; NATIVITY PLAY
f Nativité
i Natività; rappresentazione della natività
d Weihnachtsstück; Krippenspiel

214 CHRONICLE PLAY; HISTORICAL PLAY; HISTORY PLAY
f pièce historique
i commedia o tragedia storica; rappresentazione storica
d Historienstück

215 CHURCH PLAY, (MEDIEVAL)
f pièce jouée dans une église
i tragedia religiosa; commedia religiosa
d Kirchenraumspiel

216 CIRCLE; TIER
f galerie
i fila
d Rang

217 CIRCULAR FLYING EFFECT
f effet de vol circulaire
i effetto di volo circolare
d Wolkenkarussel

CIRCUS STAGE see 61 ARENA STAGE

218 CIVIC THEATRE; COMMUNITY THEATRE MUNICIPAL THEATRE
f théâtre municipal
i teatro municipale
d Stadttheater

219 CLAPHAM JUNCTION
f rides (au crayon)
i rughe (fatte con la matita)
d Rollbanken (Schminke) (sl.)

220 CLAQUE
f claque
i applauditori prezzolati; claque
d Claque

221 CLASSIC(S)
f classique
i classico
d Klassiker

222 CLEAR, to (THE STAGE)
f démonter (décor)
i sgombrare la scena
d abbauen

223 CLEAR PLEASE!; CLEAR STAGE!
f dégagez le plateau
i sgombrare la scena; fuori scena per favore!
d Bühne frei!

224 CLEAT, to
f guinder
i assicurare (al gancio)
d zusammenschnüren

225 CLEAT HOOK
f sauterelle
i gancio
d Knacken

226 CLICHÉ
f cliché
i cliché
d Klischee

227 CLIMAX
f paroxisme; noeud de l'action
i apice dell'azione
d Höhepunkt

228 CLOAK AND DAGGER DRAMA
f pièce de cape et d'épée
i rappresentazione di cappa e spada
d Mantel- und Degenstück

CLOAKROOM see 200 CHECK ROOM

229 CLOSE;
CONCLUSION
f fin; dénouement
i conclusione; fine
d Schluss

230 CLOSED;
CLOSED DOWN
f fermé
i chiuso
d geschlossen

231 CLOSET DRAMA
f pièce à lire (plus qu'à jouer)
i rappresentazione più adatta alla lettura che alla recita
d Lesedrama

232 CLOTH STORE
f réserve des toiles de fond
i riserva di sfondi
d Prospektmagazin

233 CLOUD GAUZE
f tulle à nuages
i garza che produce l'effetto delle nuvole
d Wolkenschleier

234 CLOWN
f clown
i buffone; pagliaccio; clown
d Clown

235 CLOWN SCENE
f clownerie; scène bouffonne
i scena di pagliacci
d Rüpelszene

236 COACH
f professeur; maitre
i professore
d Lehrer

COARSE see 149 BROAD

COATROOM see 200 CHECK ROOM

237 COCKTAIL DRAMA;
DRAWING-ROOM PLAY
f comédie de salon
i commedia di salotto
d Salonstück

238 COLLECTION;
STOCK
f fonds; inventaire
i scorta; inventario
d Fundus; Inventar

239 COLOUR DISCS;
"JELLIES";
COLOUR MEDIA
f gélatines; écrans colorés
i gelatina; dischi di schermi di mica
d Farbscheiben

240 COLOUR FRAMES
f porte-écrans
i porta gelatina; supporto della gelatina
d Farbschieber

COLOUR MEDIA see 239 COLOUR DISCS

241 COLOUR MUSIC CONTROL; CONSOLE
f jeu d'orgue
i comando
d Lichtklavier; Lichtorgel

242 COMEDIAN
f comique
i comico
d Komiker

243 COMEDY
f comédie
i commedia
d Komödie; Lustspiel

244 COMEDY-FARCE; FARCE; FARSE-COMEDY; FARSICAL COMEDY
f farce
i farsa
d Posse; Schwank

245 COMEDY OF HUMOUR
f comédie humoristique
i stile ricercato
d "Humour"-Komödie

246 COMEDY OF MANNERS; HIGH COMEDY
f comédie de moeurs
i commedia di maniera
d Gesellschaftskomödie; Sittenkomödie

COME ON, to, see 52 to APPEAR

247 COME TO THE FRONT, to; to STEAL THE SHOW
f porter la pièce (en effaçant les autres)
i farsi notare (a discapito degli altri)
d an die Wand spielen

248 COMIC
f comique
i buffo; comico
d komisch

249 COMIC OPERA; OPERETTA
f opérette
i operetta
d Operette

250 COMMEDIA DELL'ARTE; MASKED COMEDY
f commedia dell'arte
i commedia dell'arte
d Commedia dell'arte

251 COMMERCIAL THEATRE
f théâtre commercial
i teatro commerciale
d Geschäftstheater; Kassentheater

COMMUNITY THEATRE see 218 CIVIC THEATRE

COMPANY see 15 ACTING GROUP

COMPANY see 101 BAND

252 COMPÈRE
f présentateur
i presentatore
d Conferencier

253 COMPÈRE AT, to; to EMCEE AN EVENT (US)
f présenter
i presentare
d conferieren

254 COMPETITION
f concurrence
i concorrenza
d die Konkurrenz

255 COMPLIMENTARY TICKET; FREE TICKET
f billet de faveur

i biglietto di favore
d Freikarte

256 CONCEPTION OF A CHARACTER
f conception du personnage
i creazione del personaggio
d Rollenauffassung

257 CONCERTED ACTING; CONCERTED PLAY
f jeu concerté
i recitare in modo concertato
d konzertantes Spiel

258 CONCESSION TO THE AUDIENCE'S TASTE
f concession au goût du public
i il condiscendere al gusto del pubblico
d Konzession an den Publikumsgeschmack

CONCLUSION see 229 CLOSE

259 CONDUCTOR
f chef d'orchestre
i direttore d'orchestra
d Dirigent

CONSOLE see 241 COLOUR MUSIC CONTROL

260 CONTEMPORARY COSTUME
f costume moderne
i costume moderno
d zeitgenössisches Kostüm

261 CONTENTS
f table des matières
i indice
d Inhaltsangabe

262 CONVERSATION PIECE
f pièce de salon
i recita bassata per lo più sul dialogo e non sull' azione
d Konversationsstück

CONVERT (A BUILDING), to, see 27 to ADAPT

263 CONVEYOR BELT; ENDLESS BAND; TREADMILL
f fil continu; tapis roulant
i catena di montaggio
d laufendes Band

264 COPYRIGHT
f droits d'auteur
i "copyright"
d Urheberrecht

265 CORPUS CHRISTI PLAY
f pièce de la Fête Dieu
i rappresentazione del Corpus Domini; auto sacramental
d Fronleichnamsspiel

266 COSTUME; DRESS
f costume
i costume
d Kostüm

267 COSTUME DESIGN; COSTUME SKETCH
f maquette de costume
i disegno del costume; bozzetto del costume; schizzo del costume
d Kostümentwurf; Figurine

268 COSTUME PLAY; COSTUME PIECE
f pièce à costumes
i commedia in costume
d Kostümstück

269 COSTUMER
f décorateur-costumier
i costumista
d Kostümbildner

270 COSTUMIER'S
f maison de location de costumes
i negozio dove si affitano costumi
d Kostümleihanstalt

271 COUNTERWEIGHT
f contrepoids
i contrappeso
d Gegengewicht

272 COURT THEATRE
f théâtre de cour
i teatro di corte
d Hoftheater; Residenz-theater

273 CRAB, to
to SLATE;
to TEAR TO PIECES
f ereinter
i denigrare; screditare; criticare severamente
d verreissen

CRACK see 94 BAD JOIN

274 CRAFTSMANSHIP
f "métier"
i abilità tecnica; "mestiere"
d technisches Können

275 CRASH MACHINE;
NOISE MACHINE
f machine à faire du bruit
i macchina per (produrre) rumori
d Krachmaschine

276 CREATE A ROLE, to
f créer un rôle
i creare una parte
d eine Rolle kreieren

277 CREATIVE WORK
f travail créateur
i lavoro creativo; creazione
d schöpferische Arbeit

278 CRITIC;
CRIX (sl.);
CRICKS (sl.);
REVIEWER
f critique
i critico
d Kritiker; Rezensent

279 CRITICISM;
CRITIQUE;
REVIEW;
NOTICES
f critique; compte-rendu
i critica
d Kritik; Rezension

280 CROWD SCENE;
MASS SCENE;
MOB SCENE
f scène de foule
i scena di massa
d Massenszene

281 CROWD STAGING
f mise en scène de foules
i allestimento della scena di massa
d Masseninszenierung

282 CUE
f réplique
i battuta d'entrata; imbeccata
d Stichwort; Einsatz

283 CUE-BOUND, to be;
to be CUE-STRUCK
f être esclave du texte
i dipendere dalla giusta imbeccata
d am Stichwort kleben

284 CUE SOMEBODY, to;
to GIVE SOMEBODY THE CUE
f donner la réplique
i dare l'imbeccata; dare la parola
d jemand das Stichwort geben

CUE-STRUCK, to be, see 283 to be CUE-BOUND

285 CUP-AND-SAUCER COMEDY
f comédie de salon
i commedia di salotto
d Salonlustspiel

286 CURTAIN
f rideau
i telone
d Vorhang

287 CURTAIN CALL
f rappel
i bis
d Hervorruf

288 CURTAIN FALLS
f le rideau tombe
i cala il sipario
d Vorhang fällt

289 CURTAIN MAN
f le préposé au rideau
i siparista
d Vorhangzieher

290 CURTAIN RAISER; PRELUDE
f prologue; lever de rideau
i avanspettacolo; commedia d'apertura
d Vorspiel

291 CURTAIN RISES
f le rideau se lève
i apertura del sipario
d Vorhang geht hoch

292 CURTAINS; DRAPERIES
f rideaux; draperies
i teloni; tendaggi
d Draperie

CURTAIN WARNING SIGNAL see 158 BUZZER

293 CUT
f costière
i scanalatura
d Bodenschlitz; Freifahrtschlitz

294 CUT
f coupure
i parte soppressa
d Striche

CUT, to, see 121 to BLUE-PENCIL

CUT CLOTH see 59 ARCH

CUTTING see 122 BLUE-PENCILLING

CUT VERSION see 2 ABRIDGED VERSION

295 CYCLE OF PLAYS
f cycle de pièces
i ciclo di rappresentazione
d Dramenzyklus

296 CYCLORAMA
f cyclorama; ciel
i ciclorama
d Bühnenhimmel; Rundhorizont

297 CYCLORAMA DOME; SKY DOME
f cyclorama
i ciclorama
d Kuppenhorizont; Bühnenhimmel

298 CYCLORAMA TRACK
f patience du cyclorama
i pista per ciclorama
d Laufbahn des Horizonts

299 CYLINDRIC REVOLVING STAGE
f scène tournante cylindrique
i palcoscenico girevole cilindrico
d Drehzylinderbühne

300 DAIS;
PLATFORM
f podium; estrade
i palco; podio
d Podium

301 DANCER
f danseur; danseuse
i ballerino; ballerina
d Tänzer; Tänzerin

302 DARKNESS
f noir; obscurité
i oscurità
d Dunkel

303 DEAD-PAN (face)
f inexpressif
i impassibile; senza espressione
d ausdruckslos

304 DEAD SEASON
f morte saison
i stagione morta
d Sauregurkenzeit

305 DEAD STEAM;
LOW PRESSURE STEAM
f vapeur à basse pression
i vapore a bassa pressione
d Niederdruckdampf

306 DEBUT;
FIRST APPEARANCE ON THE STAGE
f débuts, les; début sur scène
i prima recita; debutto
d Debut; Erstauftreten; Erstes Auftreten

307 DECLAIM, to
f déclamer
i declamare
d deklamieren

308 DECLAMATORY STYLE
f style déclamatoire
i stile declamatorio
d Deklamationsstil

309 DÉCOR;
SETTING;
TRAPPINGS;
DECORATION;
STAGE SET;
SCENERY
f décor; décoration
i decorazione; scenario
d Bühnenbild; Bild; Dekorationen; Szenerie

310 DECORATIVE
f décoratif
i decorativo
d dekorativ

311 DÉCOR SIMULTANÉ;
MULTIPLE STAGING;
SIMULTANEOUS SET;
SIMULTANEOUS SETTING
f décor simultané
i scenario simultaneo
d Simultandekoration

312 DEEP STAGE
f scène profonde
i scena tanto profonda quanto larga
d tiefe Bühne

DELETE, to, see 121 to BLUE-PENCIL

313 DELIVER AN ASIDE, to
f dire en aparté
i dire un a parte
d beiseite sprechen

314 DENOUEMENT
f dénouement
i conclusione
d Lösung des Knotens

315 DEPARTMENT OF DRAMA;
INSTITUTE OF THEATRICAL STUDY;
INSTITUTE OF DRAME
f institut d'études théâtrales
i istituto di studi teatrali
d Theaterwissenschaftliches Institut

316 DEPOT;
STORAGE SPACE;
DOCK;
STORAGE ROOMS
f magasins
i deposito; magazzino
d Depot; Lagerräume

317 DEUS EX MACHINA
f deus ex machina
i deus ex machina
d deus ex machina

318 DEVELOPMENT OF CHARACTER
f progression du personnage
i sviluppo progressivo di un personaggio
d Charakterentwicklung

319 DIALECT PLAY
f pièce en dialecte
i rappresentazione dialettale
d Mundartstück

320 DIALOG(UE);
f dialogue
i dialogo
d Dialog

321 DICTION
f diction
i dizione
d Diktion

322 DIDACTIC DRAMA
f pièce didactique
i dramma didattico
d Lehrstück

323 DILETTANTE
f dilettante
i dilettante
d Dilettant

324 DIMMER
f résistance; gradateur
i oscuratore (di luce)
d Verdunkler

325 DIMMER BOARD
f tableau de commande
i commutatore delle luci
d Schalttafel

326 DIONYSIAC FESTIVALS
f dionysiaques
i baccanali; feste dionisiache
d Dionysien

327 DIRECT, to;
to STAGEMANAGE
f mettre en scène
i mettere in scena
d Regie führen

328 DIRECTION;
DIRECTING;
PRODUCTION
f mise en scène
i regia
d Regie

329 DIRECTOR (US);
PRODUCER (GB)
f metteur en scène
i regista
d Regisseur

330 DIRECTOR;
STAGE MANAGER
f metteur en scène; meneur de jeu
i direttore tecnico delle scene
d Spielleiter

331 DISGUISE
f déguisement
i travestimento
d Verkleidung

332 DISH A SCENE, to
f enlever une scène; jouer une scène à tout casser
i rovinare una scena
d eine Szene schmeissen

333 DISTORT, to
f déformer
i alterare la forma
d verzerren

334 DITHYRAMB
f dithyrambe
i ditirambo
d Dithyrambus

335 DIVA;
STAR (actress)
f diva; étoile
i diva; stella; star
d Diva

DOCK see 316 DEPOT

336 DOCTOR A PLAY, to;
to VET A PLAY (sl.);
to RE-WORK
f remanier
i rivedere un lavoro teatrale; rimaneggiare
d umarbeiten

337 DOGGEREL
f vers boîteux
i versi irregolari; versi zoppi; filastrocca
d Knüttelvers

DOMESTIC COMEDY see 133 BOURGEOIS COMEDY

338 DOMESTIC TRAGEDY
f "tragédie domestique"; drame bourgeois
i tragedia borghese
d bürgerliches Trauerspiel

339 DOUBLEDECK STAGE
f scène à deux étages
i scena a due piani
d Doppelstockbühne

340 DRAG to
f tirer
i trascinare; tracsinarsi;
d schleppen

341 DRAMA;
PLAY;
PIECE
f pièce; littérature dramatique; jeu
i rappresentazione; dramma
d Drama; Schauspiel; Spiel; Stück

342 DRAMA, the;
TREASURY OF DRAMA
f répertoire
i il teatro
d Dramengut

343 DRAMA CLUB;
DRAMA SOCIETY
f club théâtral
i club teatrale
d Theaterverein

344 DRAMATIC
f dramatique
i drammatico
d dramatisch

345 DRAMATIC SCHOOL;
THEATRE SCHOOL;
SCHOOL OF ACTING;
SCHOOL OF DRAMATIC ART
f école d'art dramatique
i scuola d'arte drammatica
d Schauspielschule

DRAMATIC SOCIETY see 15 ACTING GROUP

346 DRAMATIC TRAINING
f apprentissage dramatique; formation du comédien
i formazione artistico drammatica
d Schauspielausbildung

347 DRAMATIS PERSONAE
f les personnages
i (i) personnaggi
d Personen der Handlung

DRAMATIST see 763 PLAYWRIGHT

348 DRAMATIZATION
f dramatisation
i drammatizzazione
d Dramatisierung

349 DRAMATURGY
f dramaturgie
i drammaturgia
d Dramaturgie

DRAPERIES see 292 CURTAINS

350 DRAPERY BORDER
f frise d'Arlequin
i mantello d'Arlecchino
d Mantelsoffitte

351 DRAPING
f drapé
i tendaggio
d Faltenwurf

DRAWING POWER see 75 ATTRACTION

DRAWING-ROOM PLAY see 237 COCKTAIL DRAMA

DRESS see 266 COSTUME

352 DRESS CIRCLE
f balcon; corbeille; premier balcon
i prima balconata
d erster Rang

353 DRESSER
f habilleur; habilleuse
i vestiarista
d Ankleider(in); Garderober (in)

354 DRESSING ROOM
f loge d'artiste
i camerino
d Ankleideraum

DRESSING ROOM see 200 CHECK ROOM

355 DRESS PARADE
f présentation des costumes
i presentazione dei costumi
d Kostümprobe

356 DRESS REHEARSAL
f la couturière
i prova generale
d Hauptprobe

357 DRESS REHEARSAL, (final, last)
f générale, la (répétition)
i prova generale
d Generalprobe

358 DROP
f frise
i telone; sipario
d Hängestück

359 DROP CURTAIN
f rideau à l'allemande
i sipario; telone
d Fallvorhang

DRY UP, to, see 99 to BALLOON

360 DUAL (role)
f double rôle; deux rôles (joué par une seule personne)
i doppia parte; ruolo interpretato da una stessa persona
d Doppelrolle

361 DUD PART
f rôle ingrat; rôle sacrifié; rôle casse-cou
i parte ingrata; parte sacrificata
d Baum; Wurzen (sl.)

362 DUTCHMAN
f tasseau
i spessore
d Schlagleiste

363 EASTER PLAY
f Passion; Jeu de la Passion
i Passione
d Osterspiel

364 ECCYCLEMA
f eccyclème
i eccyclema
d Ekkyklema

365 ELABORATE, to
f travailler; mettre au point
i elaborare; mettere a punto
d ausarbeiten

366 ELECTRICIAN, (stage); LIGHTING TECHNICIAN
f éclairagiste; électricien
i elettricista
d Beleuchter

367 ELECTRICIAN'S BALCONY
f pont d'éclairage
i ponte delle luci
d Beleuchterbrücke

368 ELEVATOR STAGE; SINKING STAGE
f scène sur ascenseur
i palcoscenico mobile
d Hebebühne; Versenkbühne

369 ELIZABETHAN THEATRE
f théâtre élisabéthain
i teatro elisabettiano
d elisabethanisches Theater

370 ELOCUTION; VOICE TECHNIQUE
f technique déclamatoire
i l'arte del declamare
d Sprechtechnik

371 EMCEE; MASTER OF CEREMONIES (M.C.); HERALD
f présentateur
i maestro di cerimonia
d Ansager

EMCEE, to, see 46 to ANNOUNCE

EMCEE AN EVENT, to, see 253 to COMPÈRE AT

372 EMERGENCY EXIT
f sortie de secours
i uscita di sicurezza
d Notausgang

373 EMERGENCY LAMP
f lampe de secours
i lampada di soccorso
d Notlampe

374 EMERGENCY UNDERSTUDY; UNDERSTUDY
f doublure
i doppiatore; sostituto (in caso di emergenza); artista di reserva
d zweite Besetzung; Ersatz

ENCORE see 115 BIS

ENDLESS BAND see 263 CONVEYOR BELT

375 ENGAGEMENT
f contrat
i contratto
d Verpflichtung

376 ENGAGEMENT; "SHOP"
f engagement
i scrittura teatrale
d Engagement

377 ENGINE ROOM
f salle des machines
i sala macchine
d Maschinenraum

378 ENGLISH ACTORS (hist.); ENGLISH COMEDIANS
f les "Comédiens Anglais"
i gli attori inglesi
d Englische Komödianten

ENSEMBLE see 15 ACTING GROUP

379 ENSEMBLE PLAYING;
TEAM PLAYING;
ENSEMBLE ACTING
f jeu d'ensemble; mouvement d'ensemble
i movimento di assieme; recita di assieme; lavoro di équipe
d Ensemblespiel; Zusammenspiel

ENTER, to see 52 to APPEAR

380 ENTER A ;
A ENTERS
f A. entre en scène
i A entra in scena; entra A
d A. tritt auf

381 ENTERTAINMENT
f divertissement
i spettacolo; intermezzo
d Unterhaltung

382 ENTERTAINMENT PLAY
f un divertissement
i intermezzo
d Unterhaltungsstück

383 ENTHUSIAST:
FAN
f enthousiaste
i entusiasta
d Enthusiast

384 ENTIRE VERSION
f version intégrale
i versione integrale
d vollständige Fassung

385 ENTR'ACTE MUSIC;
INTERVAL MUSIC
f intermède musical
i musica d'intervallo
d Zwischenaktsmusik

ENTRANCE see 53 APPEARANCE

ENUNCIATION see 63 ARTICULATION

386 EPIC DRAMA
f drame épique
i dramma epico
d episches Drama

387 EPIC THEATRE (Brecht)
f théâtre épique
i teatro epico
d episches Theater

388 EPILOGUE
f épilogue
i epilogo
d Epilog

389 EPISODE
f épisode
i episodio
d Episode

390 EQUESTRIAN DRAMA
f pièce équestre
i dramma equestre
d Pferdedrama

391 EVENT
f événement
i avvenimento; evento
d Ereignis

392 EXAGGERATE, to;
to OVERACT
f charger; exagérer; en remettre
i esagerare; caricare
d chargieren; outzieren; übertreiben

393 EXIT, to
f sortir
i uscire
d abgehen

394 EXIT
f sortie
i uscita
d Abgang

395 EXITING;
ON EXIT
f en sortant
i uscendo
d im Abgehen

396 EXPERIMENTAL THEATRE
f théâtre d'essai; théâtre expérimental
i teatro sperimentale
d experimentelles Theater

397 EXPOSITION
f exposition
i esposizione
d Exposition

398 EXPRESSIONISTIC
f expressioniste
i espressionistico
d expressionistisch

399 EXTEMPORE PLAY;
IMPROPTU PLAY;
IMPROVISED PLAY
f improvisation; impromptu
i improvisazione
d Stegreifspiel

400 EXTERIOR (scene)
f décor d'extérieur
i scena d'esterno
d Exterieur

401 EXTRA;
SUPER(NUMERARY)
f figurant
i comparsa
d Statist; Statistin

402 EXTRAS;
SUPERNUMERARIES;
SUPERS
f figuration
i comparse
d Komparserie

403 EXTRAVAGANCE;
EXTRAVAGANZA
f extravagance
i stravaganza; bizzaria
d Extravaganz

404 EYEBROW PENCIL
f crayon à sourcils
i matita per le sopraciglia
d Augenbrauenstift

405 EYE SHADOW
f maquillage des paupières
i ombretto per gli occhi
d Augenschatten

406 FAÇADE
f façade
i facciata
d Fassade

407 FACIAL PLAY
f mimique
i mimica
d Mimik

408 FAIL, to;
to BE A FLOP
f faire un four
i fare fiasco
d durchfallen

409 FAILURE;
FLOP
f échec; four
i fiasco
d Durchfall; Versager

410 FAIRY PLAY;
FAIRY DRAMA
f féerie
i féerie
d Märchenspiel

411 FAIRYTALE FARCE
f féerie burlesque
i féerie; farsa burlesca
d Zauberposse

412 FAITHFUL RENDERING
f interprétation fidèle
i interpretazione fedele
d getreue Wiedergabe

413 FALSE HEROICS;
MOCK HEROICS
f pathos
i eroicomico
d falsches Pathos

414 FALSE LASHES
f faux cils
i ciglia finte
d falsche Wimpern

FAN see 383 ENTHUSIAST

415 FAN MAIL
f courrier des admirateurs
i corrispondenza (da parte degli ammiratori)
d Verehrerpost

FARCE see 244 COMEDY-FARCE

FARSE-COMEDY see 244 COMEDY-FARCE

FARSICAL COMEDY see 244 COMEDY FARCE

416 FASTEN, to;
to SECURE
f attacher; assurer
i attaccare
d sichern

417 FAT PART
f rôle à effet; rôle en or
i parte d'oro
d Bombenrolle

418 FEATURE SOMEBODY, to;
to GIVE SOMEBODY STAR-BILLING;
to GIVE SOMEBODY TOP-BILLING;
to GIVE SOMEBODY A BUILD-UP
f mettre en tête de la distribution; mettre en tête d'affiche
i dare ad un attore la preminenza sul cartellone; dare ad un attore la parte principale del manifesto; mettere in evidenza un attore
d jemand herausstellen

419 FEDERAL THEATRE;
STATE THEATRE
f théâtre d'Etat; théâtre subventionné
i teatro sovvenzionato; teatro di Stato
d Bundestheater

420 FEED;
STOOGE;
FOIL
f repoussoir
i spalla
d Stichwortbringer

421 FEED IN THE LIGHT, to
f monter la lumière
i accèndere le luci in resistènza
d einziehen (Licht)

422 FEMALE IMPERSONATOR
f travesti (homme en femme)
i travesti
d Damenimitator

423 FENCING MASTER
f maitre d'armes
i maestro di scherma
d Fechtlehrer

424 FESTIVAL
f festival
i festival
d Festspiel(e)

425 FIDELITY TO THE TEXT
f fidélité au texte
i fideltà al testo
d Texttreue

426 FILLET
f tasseau
i assicella di raccordo
d Leiste

427 FILLET
f trapillon
i tassello
d Einlage für Freifahrt-schlitz

428 FINALE
f final
i finale
d Finale

429 FINAL PERFORMANCE;
LAST PERFORMANCE
f la dernière
i ultima rappresentazione
d Schlussvorstellung

430 FINGERTIP APPLAUSE
f applaudissements polis
i applausi tiepidi
d Höflichkeitsapplaus

431 FIRE PRECAUTIONS INSPECTOR
f Inspecteur-pompier
i Ispettore dei Vigili del fuoco
d Feuerwehrinspektor

432 FIREMEN
f les pompiers de service
i pompieri
d Theaterfeuerwehr

433 FIREPROOF, to;
to FLAMEPROOF
f ignifuger
i rendere ininfiammabile
d imprägnieren

434 FIRST-AID ATTENDANT
f médecin de service
i assistente di pronto soccorso
d Theaterarzt

FIRST APPEARANCE ON THE STAGE see 306 DEBUT

435 FIRST LADY;
LEADING LADY;
LEADING WOMAN;
HEROINE;
PRINCIPAL ACTRESS;
PRINCIPAL LADY
f la protagoniste; héroine
i eroina; protagonista
d Hauptdarstellerin; Heldin

436 FIRST MAN;
LEADING MAN;
HERO;
PRINCIPAL MAN;
PRINCIPAL ACTOR
f protagoniste; héros

i eroe; protagonista; primo attore
d Hauptdarsteller; Held

437 FIRST NIGHT;
PREMIERE;
PREMIER PERFORMANCE;
OPENING NIGHT;
OPENING PERFORMANCE;
PREMIER PRESENTATION;
ORIGINAL PERFORMANCE
f première; création
i prima rappresentazione; prima recita; prima
d Premiere; Erstaufführung; Uraufführung

438 FIRST-NIGHT A PLAY, to
f créer
i dare la prima rappresentazione
d uraufführen

439 FIRST-NIGHTERS
f public de première
i pubblico della prima (rappresentazione)
d Premierenpublikum

440 FIRST READING;
READING BY THE CAST;
SCRIPT READING
f première lecture
i prima lettura
d Leseprobe

441 FITTING
f essayage
i prova (dei costumi)
d Anprobieren

442 FIT-UP;
MAKESHIFT STAGE
f scène de fortune
i palcoscenico di fortuna
d Behelfsbühne

FIT-UP see 104 BARNSTORMERS

FLAMEPROOF, to, see 433 to FIREPROOF

443 FLASH-BACK
f retour en arrière; flash-back
i flash-back
d Rückblende

444 FLATS
f châssis; ferme
i quinta
d Flachkulissen; flache Bühnenbildteile

445 FLOATS;
FOOTLIGHTS;
RAMP;
LIMELIGHT
f rampe
i luci della ribalta
d Rampe; Rampenlicht; Fusslampen; Fusslichter

FLOP see 409 FAILURE

FLOP, to be a, see 408 to FAIL

446 FLOWER WALK;
FLOWER-WAY;
HANAMICHI;
FLOWER PATH
f "chemin des fleurs"; Hanamichi du Kabuki
i sentiero dei fiori
d Blumensteg

447 FLOWN PIECE
f décor équipé aux cintres
i scena volante
d Hängedekoration

448 FLUFF, to;
to MUFF
f rater un effet; rater une scène; rater un rôle; bousiller
i sbagliare un'effetto; sbagliare una scena; sbagliare una parte; impaperarsi
d patzen (coll.)

449 FLY FLOOR
f passerelle de service
i passerella di servizio
d Arbeitsgalerie

450 FLYING EQUIPMENT;
FLYING MACHINERY
f équipe de vol
i macchinario delle centine
d Flugmaschine

451 FLYING SPACE
f les cintres
i centinatura
d Oberbühne

452 FOCUS SOMETHING BY LIGHT, to;
to SPOT;
to PICK OUT SOMEBODY OR SOMETHING
to HIT SOMEBODY OR SOMETHING (US);
to LIGHT AN ACTOR;
f éclairer (par la lumière)
i illuminare; mettere a fuoco; mettere in evidenza con la luce
d anleuchten

F.O.H. LIGHT see 459 FORE STAGE LIGHT

FOIL see 420 FEED

453 FOLK PLAY;
FOLK DRAMA
f pièce populaire
i dramma popolare
d Volksstück

454 FOLLOW SPOT
f projecteur de poursuite
i riflettore mobile
d Verfolgungsscheinwerfer

455 FOOL
f bouffon; fou
i buffone
d narr

FOOTLIGHTS see 445 FLOATS

456 FORCED;
LABOURED
f forcé
i eccessivo; non naturale; forzato
d gezwungen

457 FOREGROUND
f la face
i primo piano
d Vordergrund

458 FORE-STAGE
f proscenium; avant-scène
i proscenio; avanscena
d Proszenium; Vorbühne

459 FORE STAGE LIGHT;
FRONT OF HOUSE LIGHT;
F.O.H. LIGHT
f éclairage d'avant-scène
i proiettori d'avanscena; proiettori di sala
d Vorbühnenlicht

460 FORMALISM
f formalisme
i formalismo
d Formalismus

461 FOURTH WALL, the
f le quatrième mur
i il quarto muro
d die vierte Wand

462 FOYER;
LOUNGE
f foyer
i ridotto; foyer
d Foyer

463 FRAME BATTEN;
LATTICE BATTEN
f herse cloisonnée
i assicella di carico
d Gitterträger

FREE TICKET see 255 COMPLIMENTARY TICKET

FRONT OF HOUSE LIGHT
see 459 FORE STAGE LIGHT

464 FULL HOUSE
f salle pleine
i sala piena; tutto esaurito
d volles Haus

465 FULL-LENGTH PLAY
f sans equiv. (pièce faisant la durée du spectacle)
i pezzo unico (dello spettacolo)
d abendfüllendes Stück

466 FULL LIGHTING, to use
f faire plein feu
i utilizzare tutte le illuminazioni; illuminare completamente
d ausleuchten

467 FULL MASK
f masque complet; masque entier
i maschera completa; maschera intera
d Vollmaske

FUNNY MAN see 150 BUFFOON

468 FURNITURE COLLECTION
f réserve des meubles
i raccolta di mobili; collezione di mobili
d Möbelfundus

FUSTIAN see 125 BOMBAST

469 GAIT
f allure; démarche
i passo; portamento; andatura
d Gangart

470 GALA PERFORMANCE
f représentation de gala
i rappresentazione di gala
d Galavorstellung

471 GALLERY;
UPPER BALCONY
f galerie; paradis
i galleria
d Galerie

472 GALLERY, to play to the
f jouer pour la galerie
i recitare per la galleria; cercare di incontrare il gusto del grosso pubblico
d für die Galerie spielen

GAP see 94 BAD JOIN

473 GARISH;
GAUDY;
MAWKISH;
TAWDRY;
TRASHY
f de mauvais goût; clinquant
i di cattivo gusto; senza valore
d kitschig

474 GATE MONEY
f prix des places
i prezzo d'entrata
d Eintrittsgeld

GAUDY see 473 GARISH

475 GESTICULATE, to
f gesticular
i gesticolare
d gestikulieren

476 GESTURE
f geste
i gesto; il gestire
d Gebärde; Geste

477 GET A ROUND AT ONE'S ENTRANCE, to
f être applaudi à son entrée; faire une entrée
i raccogliere applausi all' entrata; ricevere un applauso all'entrata in scena
d Empfangsapplaus erhalten

478 GET INTO THE SKIN OF ONE'S ROLE, to;
to IDENTIFY ONESELF WITH ONE'S ROLE
f s'identifier; entrer dans la peau du personnage
i identificarsi col personaggio; entrare nello spitiro del personaggio; immedesimarsi nel personaggio
d einswerden mit der Rolle; sich hineinknien; in die Rolle hineinschlüpfen

479 GET OVER THE FOOTLIGHTS, to
f passer la rampe
i passare la ribalta; stabilire un rapporto con il pubblico
d über die Rampe gehen; ankommen

480 GHOST THRILLER
f sans équiv. (pièce à fantômes)
i thriller; dramma di fantasmi; spettacolo di fantasmi
d Gespensterstück

481 GIVE (A PLAY), to;
to OFFER;
to PRESENT;
to PRODUCE;
to PUT ON;
to PERFORM;
to STAGE
f représenter; monter; mettre en scène

i presentare; mettere in scena
d aufführen; inszenieren

GIVE SOMEBODY A BUILD-UP, to, see 418 to FEATURE SOMEBODY

GIVE SOMEBODY STAR-BILLING, to, see 418 to FEATURE SOMEBODY

482 GIVE SOMEBODY THE BIRD, to;
to HISS (AND BOO) A PLAY
f siffler; huer
i fischiare
d auspfeifen

GIVE SOMEBODY THE CUE, to, see 284 to CUE SOMEBODY

GIVE SOMEBODY TOP-BILLING see 418 to FEATURE SOMEBODY

483 GIVE THE CUE, to
f souffler le début de la réplique
i dare l'imbeccata,
d Anschlag geben

484 GLOVE PUPPET THEATRE
f théâtre de marionnettes à gaine
i teatro di marionette; teatro di fantocci
d Handpuppentheater

485 GLUE, to
f coller
i incollare
d leimen

486 GO!
f allez-y!
i azione!
d Los!

487 GOAT SONG
f chant du bouc
i tragedia
d Bocksgesang

488 'GO MUSIC HALL', to;
to 'GO VARIEY'
f dégénérer en music-hall; tourner au music-hall
i andare a finire al music hall; buttarsi al music hall
d tingeln

489 GO ON FOR SOMEBODY, to;
to UNDERSTUDY
f remplacer au pied levé
i doppiare; sostituire
d einspringen

490 GO ON THE STAGE, to
f devenir comédien; se destiner au théâtre
i divenire attore
d Schauspieler werden

491 GONG
f gong
i gong
d Gong

492 GOOD SIGHT LINES, A SCENE HAS
f le décor n'a pas de découvertes
i la scena à visibile da ogni parte
d Dekoration hat Deckung

"GO VARIETY", to, see 488 to "GO MUSIC HALL"

GRAND AIRS see 611 MANNERISMS

493 GRAND DAME
f grand premier rôle féminin (au théâtre de salon)
i principale parte femminile
d Salondame

494 GRATE;
LATTICE
f grille

i graticcia; grata
d Gitter

495 GREASEPAINT;
MAKE-UP
f fard; maquillage
i trucco
d Schminke

496 GREEN ROOM
f foyer des artistes
i sala di attesa degli artisti
d Konversationszimmer

497 GRID;
GRID FLOOR
f gril
i graticcia
d Schnürboden; Rollenboden

498 GRIMACE
f grimace; mine
i smorfia
d Grimasse

499 GRIP HAND;
STAGE HAND;
STAGE CREW
f machiniste
i macchinista
d Bühnenarbeiter

500 GROTESQUE
f grotesque
i grottesco
d Groteske

501 GROTESQUE MASK
f masque de farce
i maschera grottesca
d Groteskmaske

502 GROUND PLAN
f plan; plantation (du décor)
i costruzione della scena;
piano
d Grundriss; Plan

503 GUEST PERFORMANCE;
STAGIONE PERFORMANCE
f spectacle de tournée
i spettacolo rappresentato
da una compagnia in preser
tazione
d Gastspiel

504 GUIDE;
TRACK
f patience
i guida
d Führung (Seilzüge)

505 HAIRDRESSER
f coiffeur
i parrucchiere
d Friseur

506 HAIRSTYLES
f coiffures
i pettinature; acconciature
d Frisuren

507 HALF CHORUS
f demi-choeur
i semi coro
d Halbchor

508 HALF MASK
f demi-masque
i semi maschera
d Halbmaske

HALL see 81 AUDITORIUM

509 HALL STAGE
f salle dotée d'une scène
i sala con una scena
d Saalbühne

510 HAM ACTOR
f acteur minable
i attore da strapazzo
d Schmierenschauspieler

HANAMICHI see 446 FLOWER WALK

HAND see 54 APPLAUSE

511 HAND PROPS
f accessoire personnel
i accessori
d Handrequisit

512 HANG ON TO THE PROMPTER, to
f se cramponner au souffleur
i aggrapparsi al suggeritore
d am Kasten kleben

513 HAPPY ENDING
f dénouement heureux
i conclusione a lieto fine
d Happyend

514 HEAD FLY MAN
f chef cintrier
i addetto alle centine
d Schnürbodenmeister

515 HEAD OF WORKROOMS
f chef des ateliers
i direttore degli studi
d Werkstättenleiter

516 HEAD-PRODUCED VOICE; HEAD VOICE
f voix de tête
i voce di testa
d Kopfstimme

HEAVY FATHER see 681 OLD MAN

HEAVY MOTHER see 682 OLD WOMAN

HERALD see 371 EMCEE

HERO see 436 FIRST MAN

517 HEROIC TRAGEDY
f tragédie héroique
i tragedia eroica
d heroische Tragödie

518 HEROICS
f pathos
i eroicomico
d Pathos

HEROINE see 435 FIRST LADY

519 HESSIAN
f jute; toile à sac
i tela di iuta fine
d Rupfen

HIGH COMEDY see 246 COMEDY OF MANNERS

HIGH TRAGIC BOOT see 156 BUSKIN

HISS (AND BOO) A PLAY, to, see 482 to GIVE SOMEBODY THE BIRD

520 HISTORICAL ACCURACY
f fidélité
i esattezza storica
d Geschichtstreue

HISTORICAL PLAY see 214 CHRONICLE PLAY

HISTORY PLAY see 214 CHRONICLE PLAY

HISTRIONIC see 20 ACTOR-LIKE

521 HIT;
SUCCESS
f succès; pièce à succès; un "tabac"
i successo; recita di successo
d Erfolgsstück; Zugstück; Reisser (sl.)

HIT SOMEBODY OR SOMETHING, to, see 452 to FOCUS

522 HORROR TRAGEDY
f tragédie sanglante
i tragedia dell'orrore
d Greueltragödie

HOUSE see 81 AUDITORIUM

523 "HOUSE FULL";
SOLD OUT
f complet; à guichets fermés
i tutto esaurito; esaurito
d ausverkauft

524 HOUSE LIGHTS
f lumières de la salle
i luci della sala
d Saallichter

525 HOUSE SEAT
f place de service
i posto di favore
d Dienstplatz; Dienstsitz

526 HUMOUR OF CHARACTER
f comique de caractère
i senza equivalente
d Charakterkomik

527 IAMBUS
f iambe
i giambo
d Jambus

IDENTIFY ONESELF WITH ONE'S ROLE, to, see 478 to GET INTO THE SKIN OF ONE'S ROLE

528 ILLUSIONISTIC STAGE; REPRESENTATIONAL STAGE
f scène à principe illusioniste; (scène à l'italienne)
i scena a principio illusionista; scena all'italiana
d Illusionsbühne

529 IMPERSONATOR
f imitateur
i imitatore
d Imitator

530 IMPRESARIO
f imprésario
i impresario
d Impresario

IMPROMPTU PLAY see 399 EXTEMPORE PLAY

IMPROVISE, to, see 29 to AD-LIB

IMPROVISED PLAY see 399 EXTEMPORE PLAY

531 INCIDENTAL BALLET
f intermède dansant; divertissement
i intermezzo di danza
d Balletteinlage

532 INCIDENTAL MUSIC
f musique de scène
i musica di sottofondo
d Begleitmusik

533 INCLINED PLANE; RAMP
f pente; plan incliné
i ribalta; piano inclinato
d Schräge

534 INDEPENDENT THEATRE
f le Théâtre Libre
i teatro libero; teatro indipendente
d Freie Bühne

535 INDICATE, to (A MOVEMENT OR METHOD)
f indiquer un mouvement
i indicare un movimento
d markieren

536 INDIRECT LIGHTING
f éclairage indirect
i illuminazione indiretta
d indirekte Beleuchtung

537 INDIVIDUAL REHEARSAL
f répétition individuelle
i prova individuale
d Einzelprobe

538 INGENUE
f ingénue
i ingenua
d Naive

539 INSTALLATION
f mise en place arrangement
i assediamento; collocazione
d Einrichtung

INSTITUE OF DRAMA see 315 DEPARTMENT OF DRAMA

INSTITUTE OF THEATRICAL STUDY see 315 DEPARTMENT OF DRAMA

540 INTERIOR (SCENE)
f décor d'intérieur
i scena d'interni
d Interieur

541 INTERLUDE
f interlude; intermède
i intermezzo
d Interludium; Zwischenspiel

INTERMISSION see 25 ACT WAIT

INTERMISSION BELL see 103 BAR BELL

542 INTERMISSION SIGNAL
f signal d'entr'acte
i segnale d'avviso
d Pausenzeichen

543 INTERPRETATIVE ART; PERFORMING ART
f art dramatique
i arte drammatica; arte del recitare
d darstellende Kunst

544 INTERRUPT, to
f interrompre
i interrompere
d unterbrechen

INTERVAL see 25 ACT WAIT

INTERVAL MUSIC see 385 ENTR'ACT MUSIC

545 IN THE GODS (coll.)
f au Paradis; au poulailler
i in loggione; in piccionaia
d am Olymp (coll.); am Juchhe

546 IN THE PLAY, to be
f être distribué; participer
i avere un ruolo
d mitspielen

547 IN THE WINGS
f en coulisse
i nelle quinte
d in den Kulissen

548 INTIMATE THEATRE
f théâtre intime; théâtre de poche
i teatro intimo
d intimes Theater

549 INTONATION
f ton; intonation
i tono; intonazione
d Tonfall

550 INTRIGUE
f pièce à intrigue
i intreccio
d Intrigenstück

INTRODUCE, to, see 46 to ANNOUNCE

551 IN UNISON
f à l'unisson
i all'unisono; in armonia
d unisono

ITINERANT PLAYERS see 104 BARNSTORMERS

"JELLIES" see 239 COLOUR DISCS

552 JESSNER STAIRS
f équipement à plateformes et escaliers (à la manière de Jessner)
i scale Jessner
d Jessnertreppen

JESTER see 150 BUFFOON

553 JESUIT DRAMA
f théâtre des Jésuites
i teatro dei Gesuiti
d Jesuitenbühne

554 JOIN BETWEEN FLATS
f charnière; jointure; articulation (de chassis)
i cerniere dei fondali; giunture dei fondali
d Stoss

555 JUGGLER; PRESTIDIGITATOR
f prestidigitateur; jongleur
i prestigiatore; prestidigitatore; giocoliere
d Gaukler

556 JUMP LINES, to
f sauter (du texte)
i saltare delle battute; saltare delle linee; saltare delle righe
d auslassen (Zeilen); springen

557 JUVENILE LADY
f héroine; jeune première dramatique
i eroina
d jugendliche Heldin; jugendliche Liebhaberin

558 KEY SCENE
- f scène-clef
- i scena chiave
- d Schlüsselszene

559 KILL, to (sl.)
- f couper (l'éclairage, un projecteur)
- i smorzare
- d ausschalten (Scheinwerfer)

560 KILL A SCENE, to
- f bouleverser (une mise en scène)
- i rovinare una scena
- d umwerfen

561 KNOCK-ABOUT COMEDY; KNOCK-AND-TUMBLE COMEDY; SLAPSTICK COMEDY
- f chahut; chambard
- i farsa grossolana
- d Klamauk

562 LABEL, to
f fixer dans un emploi
i stereotipare
d abstempeln (einen Schauspieler für ein bestimmtes Fach)

LABOURED see 456 FORCED

563 LACHRYMOSE COMEDY; SENTIMENTAL COMEDY
f comédie larmoyante
i commedia lacrimosa
d Rührkomödie

564 LACHRYMOSE DRAMA; SENTIMENTAL DRAMA; SOB-DRAMA; TEAR-JERKER (sl.); TWO-HANDKERCHIEF DRAMA (sl.)
f mélodrame
i melodramma
d Rührstück

LAST PERFORMANCE see 429 FINAL PERFORMANCE

565 LATE-COMERS WILL NOT BE ADMITTED
f les portes seront fermées au lever du rideau; les retardataires ne sont pas admis dans la salle après le début du spectacle
i le porte saranno chiuse all'apertura del sipario; i ritardatarii non potranno entrare nella sala quando lo spettacolo ha avuto inizio
d Zuspätkommende werden nicht eingelassen

LATTICE see 494 GRATE

LATTICE BATTEN see 463 FRAME BATTEN

LATTICE BOX see 107 BASKET BOX

566 LAUGH
f un rire (dans la salle)
i riso
d Lacher

567 LAY IT ON WITH A TROWEL, to
f charger; en remettre
i esagerare; adulare grossolanamente
d auf die Tube drücken (sl.)

568 LEAD; LEADING ROLE; LEADING PART
f rôle principal
i parte principale
d Hauptrolle

LEADING LADY see 435 FIRST LADY

LEADING MAN see 436 FIRST MAN

LEADING WOMAN see 435 FIRST LADY

569 "LEARN THE ROPES", to
f se mettre dans le rôle; apprendre les ficelles du théâtre
i imparare i trucchi del mestiere; imparare i trucchi del teatro
d sich freispielen

570 LEAVE A PASSAGE, to
f libérer un passage
i lasciare un passaggio
d Durchgang freilassen

571 LECTERN; READING DESK
f table; pupitre (de conférencier)
i leggio
d Vortragstisch; Vortragspult

572 LESSEE;
TENANT
f possesseur du bail
i locatario
d Pächter

573 LETTER PERFECT, to be;
to be WORD PERFECT
f être sûr de son texte
i essere esatto nei minimi particolari
d textsicher sein

LETTICE BOX see 107 BASKET BOX

574 LIBRETTIST
f librettiste
i lebirettista
d Librettist

575 LIBRETTO;
LINES;
TEXT;
SCRIPT
f texte; livret
i testo; libretto
d Libretto; Text

576 LICENSE
f licence; concession
i concessione; permesso
d Konzession

577 LIFELESS PLAYING
f "bide"
i recita senza vita; recita insignificante
d kalter Kaffee

LIGHT AN ACTOR, to, see 452 to FOCUS

LIGHT FARCE see 132 BOULEVARD COMEDY

578 LIGHTING
f éclairage
i illuminazione
d Beleuchtung

579 LIGHTING BOOTH
f cabine électrique
i cabina dell'elettricista
d Beleuchterkabine

580 LIGHTING CONTROL
f jeu d'orgue
i quadro di commando elettrico
d Bühnenregler

581 LIGHTING DIRECTOR
f régisseur des éclairages
i direttore delle luci
d Beleuchtungsingenieur

582 LIGHTING EFFECT
f effet de lumière
i effetto di luce
d Lichteffekt

583 LIGHTING PLOT
f conduite d'éclairage; plan des éclairages
i piano d'illuminazione
d Beleuchtungsplan

584 LIGHTING REHEARSAL
f réglage des lumières
i prova dell'illuminazione
d Beleuchtungsprobe

LIGHTING TECHNICIAN see 366 (stage) ELECTRICIAN

585 LIGHT TOWER
f tourelle des projecteurs
i torretta delle luci
d Beleuchtungsturm

LIMELIGHT see 445 FLOAT

LINES see 575 LIBRETTO

586 LIP PENCIL;
LIPSTICK
f rouge à lèvres
i rossetto
d Lippenstift

587 LITERARY DIRECTOR
f "dramaturge"; conseiller littéraire
i consigliere letterario
d Dramaturg

588 LOADING PLATFORM
f pont de service
i passerella di servizio
d Arbeitsbrücke

589 LOBBY
f couloir; promenoir
i lòggia
d Wandelgang

590 LOCAL COLOUR
f couleur locale
i colore locale
d Lokalkolorit

591 LOCALE;
SCENE OF ACTION
f lieu de l'action
i luogo dell'azione
d Schauplatz

592 LOSE ONE'S IDENTITY IN THE ROLE, to
f s'oublier dans le rôle
i immedesimarsi; identificarsi col personaggio
d aufgehen in der Rolle

LOUNGE see 462 FOYER

593 LOVER
f amouroux; amoureuse
i innamorato; innamorata
d Liebhaber; Liebhaberin

LOW see 149 BROAD

LOW PRESSURE STEAM see 305 DEAD STEAM

594 LYRE-SHAPED
f en forme de lyre
i a forma di cetra; a forma di lira
d lyraförmig

595 LYRICS
f paroles d'un chant
i arie; parti cantate
d Liedtext(e)

596 MACHINE STAGE;
MECHANIZED STAGE
f théâtre à machinerie
i scena meccanizzata
d Maschinentheater; technisierte Bühne

597 MACHINERY
f machinerie
i attrezzatura; macchinario
d Maschinerie

598 MACHINERY OF THE FLIES
f machinerie des cintres
i macchinario della centinatura
d Obermaschinerie

599 MACHINIST
f machiniste
i macchinista di scena
d Maschinist

600 MAIN ACTION;
MAIN PLOT
f action principale
i azione principale
d Haupthandlung

MAIN CHARACTER see 180 CENTRAL FIGURE

MAKE AN ENTRANCE, to, see 52 to APPEAR

601 MAKE A POINT, to
f faire un gag; faire un effet; souligner un effet
i fare un effetto; sottolineare un effetto
d eine Pointe landen

602 MAKESHIFT ARRANGEMENT;
MAKESHIFT SOLUTION
f expédient; pis-aller; moyen de fortune
i soluzione di ripiego
d Notbehelf

MAKESHIFT STAGE see 442 FIT-UP

603 MAKE UP, to
f maquiller
i truccare; truccarsi
d Maske machen

MAKE-UP see 495 GREASEPAINT

604 MAKE-UP ARTIST
f maquilleur; réalisateur des masques
i truccatore
d Maskenbildner; Schminkmeister

605 MAKE-UP BOX
f boite à maquillage
i scatola per il trucco
d Schminkschatulle

606 MAKE-UP JAR;
MAKE-UP POT
f pot de maquillage
i vasetto per il trucco
d Schminktiegel

607 MAKE-UP TABLE
f table à maquillage; tablette à maquillage
i tavoletta per il trucco
d Schminktisch

608 MANAGEMENT;
RÉGIME
f direction
i direzione
d Direktion

609 MANAGING DIRECTOR
f Directeur d'un théâtre subventionné
i amministratore
d Intendant

610 MANNERISM
f maniérisme
i manierismo
d Manierismus

611 MANNERISMS;
GRAND AIRS
f extravagances; poses

i stravaganza
d Allüren

612 MANSION (medieval theatre)
f mansion
i mansione
d Mansion

613 MARIONETTE THEATRE; STRING PUPPET THEATRE; PUPPET THEATRE
f théâtre de marionnettes
i teatro delle marionette
d Marionettentheater; Fadenbühne; Puppentheater

614 MARRIAGE DRAMA
f pièce se rapportant aux problèmes du couple
i commedia (o tragedia) matrimoniale
d Ehedrama

615 MASK, to
f masquer
i mascherare
d maskieren; verdecken

616 MASK
f masque
i maschera
d Maske

MASKED COMEDY see 250 COMMEDIA DELL'ARTE

617 MASQUE
f masque
i "masque"
d Maskenstück

618 MASQUERADE
f mascarade
i mascherata
d Maskerade

MASS SCENE see 280 CROWD SCENE

619 MASTER CARPENTER
f chef machiniste
i capo falegname
d Bühnenmeister

MASTER OF CEREMONIES see 371 EMCEE

MASTIC see 955 SPIRIT GUM

620 MATINEE
f matinée
i matinée; rappresentazione diurna
d Matinee; Nachmittags-vorstellung

MAWKISH see 473 GARISH

621 MEANS OF ENTRANCE
f accès; entrée
i possibilità di entrata
d Auftrittsmöglichkeit

622 MEMORIZE, to
f apprendre par coeur
i imparare a memoria
d auswendig lernen

MERRY ANDREW see 150 BUFFOON

623 MESSAGE
f signification; contenu (d'une pièce)
i messaggio
d Aussage

624 MESSENGER
f messager
i messaggero
d Bote

625 MESSENGER'S SPEECH
f tirade du messager
i discorso del messaggero
d Botenbericht

626 METALLIC VOICE; STEELY VOICE
f voix métallique

i voce metallica
d metallisches Organ

627 METHOD ACTING
f méthode des actions physiques; méthode inventée et élaborée par Stanislavsky
i messa in scena (secondo il metodo di Stanislawskij)
d Spiel nach dem Stanislawskij-System

628 MIDDLE COMEDY (Greek Theatre)
f "Comédie Moyenne" (Théâtre Grec)
i Commedia Media (Teatro Greco)
d Mittlere Komödie (Griech. Th.)

629 MID-STAGE
f centre de la scène
i centro della scena
d Mittelgrund

630 MILK THE APPLAUSE, to; to PLAY FOR APPLAUSE
f faire l'appel du pied
i recitare per la galleria
d Applaus schinden

631 MIME
f mimodrame
i azione scenica mimata
d Mimusspiel

632 MIMIC ACTOR; MIME
f mime
i mimo
d Mimusspieler; Mime

633 MINOR PART
f rôle secondaire
i parte secondaria
d Nebenrolle

634 MIRACLE PLAY
f miracle
i miracolo
d Legendenspiel; Mirakelspi

635 MISCAST
f mal distribué
i sbaglio di distribuzione
d falsch besetzt

636 MISCASTING
f erreur de distribution
i sbaglio di distribuzione; errore di distribuzione
d Fehlbesetzung

637 MISS, to
f manquer
i mancare
d verpassen

638 MISS AN ENTRANCE, to
f manquer son entrée
i mancare la (propria) entrata
d den Auftritt verpassen

639 MISS A POINT, to; to SPOIL AN EFFECT
f manquer un effet
i mancare un effetto; sbagliare un effetto; rovinare un effetto
d eine Pointe töten

MOB SCENE see 280 CROWD SCENE

MOCK HEROICS see 413 FALSE HEROICS

640 MODEL, to
f modeler; faconner; fabriquer
i modellare; disegnare
d kaschieren

641 MODEL
f maquette
i modellino; miniatura
d Modell

642 MODELLED SET
f décor(ation) plastique
i modellino della scena; plastico
d plastische Dekoration

643 MODERN DRESS, HAMLET IN
f costumes modernes, Hamlet en
i costumi moderni, Amleto in
d Frack, "Hamlet" im

644 MONODRAMA
f pièce à un personnage
i monodramma; monologo drammattico
d Monodrama; Einpersonenstück

645 MONOLOGUE; SOLILOQUY
f monologue
i monologo
d Monolog

646 MONOTONOUS
f monotone
i monotono
d monoton

647 MOOD EFFECT
f effet d'atmosphère
i effetto suggestivo; effetto di sensibilità; effetto d'emozione
d Stimmungseffekt

648 MORALITY
f moralité
i moralità
d Moralität

649 MORRIS DANCER
f danseur de morisque
i danzatore di morris
d Moriskentänzer

650 MOUNT, to
f décorer
i costruire (una scena); montare (una scena)
d ausstatten

651 MOUSTACHE
f moustache
i baffi
d Schnurrbart

652 MOVE (in stage directions), a
f passage
i passaggio
d Gang

MUFF, to, see 448 to FLUFF

653 MUG, to
f faire des grimaces
i fare una smorfia
d Grimassen schneiden

654 MULTIPLE STAGE; SIMULTANEOUS STAGE
f scène simultanée
i scena a decoro simultaneo
d Simultanbühne

MULTIPLE STAGING see 311 DECOR SIMULTANE

655 MUMMERY
f mascarade
i mimo
d Mummenschanz

MUNICIPAL THEATRE see 218 CIVIC THEATRE

656 MUSICAL ACCOMPANIMENT
f accompagnement musical
i accompagnamento musicale
d Begleitung

657 MUSICAL ARRANGEMENT
f arrangement musical
i accompagnamento musicale
d musikalische Einrichtung

658 MUSICAL COMEDY
f comédie musicale; operette
i operetta
d Singspiel

659 MUSIC HALL; VARIETY
- f varietés
- i varietà
- d Varieté

660 MUSIC HALL
- f music hall
- i music hall
- d Music Hall

661 MY LORD, THE CARRIAGE WAITS
- f la voiture de Monsieur est avancée
- i Altezza, la vettura à pronta
- d die Pferde sind gesattelt

662 MYSTERY
- f mystère
- i mistero
- d Mysterienspiel

663 NAME PART;
NAME ROLE;
TITLE ROLE
f rôle du titre
i ruolo del personaggio che da il nome alla rappresentazione
d Titelrolle

664 NARRATOR
f récitant; narrateur
i narratore
d Erzähler

665 NATIONAL THEATRE
f théâtre national
i teatro nazionale
d Nationaltheater

666 NATIVE DRAMA
f théâtre de terroir
i teatro di una nazione
d bodenständiges Drama

NATIVITY PLAY see 213 CHRISTMAS PLAY

NATURAL GIFT see 1020 TALENT

667 NATURALISTIC
f naturaliste
i naturalistico
d naturalistisch

668 NEO-CLASSIC(AL)
f néo-classique
i neo classico
d neoklassizistisch

669 NERVES;
STAGE FRIGHT
f trac
i panico; paura
d Lampenfieber

670 NEW COMEDY (Greek theatre)
f "Nouvelle Comédie" (Théâtre Grec)
i Nuova Commedia (Teatro Greco)
d Neue Komödie (Griech. Theater)

671 NO-GAKU (nó-plays)
f Nô (théâtre japonais)
i Nô (teatro giapponese)
d Noh-Spiele

NOISE MACHINE see 275 CRASH MACHINE

672 NOISES OFF;
OFF-STAGE SOUND EFFECTS
f bruits de coulisse
i rumori dietro le quinte; voci tra le quinte
d Nebengeräusche

673 NON-MUSICAL DRAMA;
STRAIGHT PLAY
f pièce dramatique
i componimento drammatico; componimento serio
d Sprechdrama; Sprechstück

674 NO PERFORMANCE
f relâche
i riposo
d "keine Vorstellung"

675 NOSE PUTTY
f pâte à nez
i impasto per il naso
d Nasenkitt

NOTICES see 279 CRITICISM

676 NUANCE;
SHADE
f nuance
i sfumatura
d Nuance

677 NUANCED
f nuancé
i sfumato
d nuanciert

678 OBLIQUE WINGS
f coulisses obliques
i quinte oblique
d Winkelkulissen

679 OBSCURE PASSAGE
f passage obscur
i passaggio oscuro nel testo
d dunkle Textstelle

OFFER, to, see 481 to GIVE (a play)

OFF-STAGE SOUND EFFECTS see 672 NOISES OFF

680 OLD COMEDY (Greek theatre)
f Comédie Anciennce (théâtre Grec)
i commedia antica (teatro greco)
d Alte Komödie (Griech. Theater)

681 OLD MAN; HEAVY FATHER
f père noble; vieillard
i vegliardo; venerando
d Heldenvater

682 OLD WOMAN; HEAVY MOTHER
f duègne; vieille dame
i veneranda
d Heldenmutter

683 ON, SHAKESPEARE IS
f on joue du Shakespeare
i si recita Shakespeare; si da Shakespeare
d man spielt Shakespeare

684 ON CUE
f à la réplique; sur la réplique
i al segnale
d aufs Stichwort

685 ONE-ACT PLAY; ONE-ACTER
f pièce en un acte
i commedia (o tragedia) in un atto; rappresentazione in un atto
d Einakter

686 ONE-SET PLAY
f pièce à décor unique
i commedia ad unico decoro; tragedia ad unico decoro
d Durchspieler

ON EXIT see 395 EXITING

687 ON STAGE!
f en scène
i in scena
d Auf die Bühne!

688 ON THE BOOK, to be
f souffler
i suggerire
d soufflieren; einsagen

689 ON THE MARKS
i ai segni
d auf Termin

690 ON THE ROAD; ON TOUR
f en tournée
i in tournée
d auf Tournee

691 ON THESE LINES
f sur ces mots; sur cette réplique (pour indiquer ce qui est alors à faire)
i su questa traccia; su queste parole
d bei diesen Worten

692 ON THE STAGE
f sur scène
i sul palcoscenico; sulla scena
d auf dem Theater

ON TOUR see 690 ON THE ROAD

693 O.P.;
STAGE RIGHT
f côté jardin
i a destra del palcoscenico
d rechts vom Schauspieler

OPEN-AIR PERFORMANCE see 33 ALFRESCO PERFORMANCE

694 OPEN-AIR THEATRE;
OUTDOOR THEATRE
f théâtre de plein air
i teatro all'aperto
d Freilichttheater

695 OPENING NIGHT (of the season)
f la première de la saison
i prima rappresentazione
d Eröffnungsvorstellung

OPENING NIGHT see 437 FIRST NIGHT

OPENING PERFORMANCE see 437 FIRST NIGHT

696 OPEN STAGE
f théâtre en rond
i scena nuda, con solo alcuni elementi decorativi
d Raumbühne

OPERETTA see 249 COMIC OPERA

697 ORCHESTRA
f orchestra; orchestre
i orchestra
d Orchestra; Orchester

698 ORCHESTRA PIT
f fosse d'orchestre
i fossa dell'orchestra; golfo mistico (nel teatro lirico)
d Orchesterraum

699 ORDER OF SCENES
f enchainement
i successione delle scene
d Szenenfolge

ORIGINAL PERFORMANCE see 437 FIRST NIGHT

OUTDOOR THEATRE see 694 OPEN-AIR THEATRE

700 OUT OF CHARACTER, to be
f être à côté du personnage
i uscire dal personaggio
d aus der Rolle fallen

OUT-OF-DOOR PERFORMANCE see 33 ALFRESCO PERFORMANCE

701 OVATION
f ovation
i ovazione
d Ovation

OVERACT, to, see 392 to EXAGGERATE

702 OVER-REHEARSED
f trop répété; trop su
i troppo ripetuto
d überprobiert

703 OVERTURE
f ouverture
i preludia; apertura
d Ouvertüre

704 PAD
f capitonnage; rembourrage
i imbottitura
d Watton

705 PAGEANT
f parade
i parata; processione
d Festzug

706 PAINT ROOM
f atelier de peinture
i studio del pittore
d Malersaal

707 PANATROPE (US);
SOUND MIXING TABLE (GB)
f table de mixage
i tavola di missaggio
d Mischpult

708 PANTOMIME;
PANTO (sl.)
f pantomime; revue-féerie
i pantomima
d Pantomime; Märchenrevue; Zauberstück

709 "PAPERED" HOUSE
f salle d'invités
i sala piena di biglietti di favore
d "wattiertes" Haus

710 PAPER SNOW
f neige de papier
i neve di carta
d Papierschnitzelschnee

711 PAPIER-MÂCHÉ
f papier mâché
i cartapesta
d Papiermaché

712 PARABASIS
f parabase
i parabasi
d Parabase

713 PARALLEL;
ROSTRUM
f praticable
i praticable
d Podest

714 PARAPET;
RAILING
f balustrade; main-courante rampe (des balcons)
i balaustra; parapetto
d Brüstung; Geländer

715 PARODY
f parodie
i parodia
d Parodie

716 PART;
RÔLE
f rôle
i parte; ruolo
d Rolle

717 PART IN A NON-MUSICAL PLAY;
STRAIGHT PART;
SPEAKING PART
f rôle parlé
i parte parlata
d Sprechrolle

718 PASSAGE
f passage
i passaggio; brano
d Stelle

719 PASS DOOR
f porte de fer
i porta del palcoscenico; porta di servizio
d Verbindungstür

720 PASSION PLAY
f Jeu de la Passion
i rappresentazione della Passione
d Passionsspiel

721 PASTEBORD (sl.);
TICKET
f billet
i biglietto teatrale
d Theaterkarte

722 PASTORALE
f pastorale
i pastorale
d Pastorale

723 PASTORAL PLAY
f pastorale
i rappresentazione pastorale
d Schäferspiel

724 PATRON;
REGULAR
f habitué
i frequentatore abituale
d Stammsitzinhaber

PAUSE see 25 ACT WAIT

725 PAUSE FOR EFFECT
f temps (prendre un temps)
i pausa piena d'effetto
d Kunstpause

726 PEASANT DRAMA;
PEASANT PLAY;
RUSTIC DRAMA
f pièce paysanne
i rappresentazione a carattere contadinesco
d Bauernstück

727 PEDESTAL
f piédestal; socle
i piedestallo
d Postament

728 PEEP HOLE
f oeil
i feritoia
d Guckscharte

729 PEEP-SHOW;
PICTURE (FRAME) STAGE
f scène à l'italienne
i scena all'italiana
d Guckkastenbühne

730 PENNY-GAFF
f troupe de quatre sous
i compagnia da quattro soldi
d Schmiere

731 PERCH SPOT;
TORMENTOR SPOT
f projecteur d'avant-scène
i proiettore di proscenio
d Proszeniumscheinwerfer

PERFORM, to, see 8 to ACT
PERFORM, to, see 481 to GIVE (A PLAY)

732 PERFORMANCE;
SHOW;
PRESENTATION;
THEATRICALS
f représentation
i rappresentazione
d Aufführung; Leistung; Vorstellung

733 PERFORMER;
PLAYER
f comédien; interprète
i attore; interprete
d Darsteller

PERFORMING ART see 543 INTERPRETATIVE ART

734 PERFORMING RIGHTS;
STAGE RIGHTS
f droits de représentation
i diritti di rappresentazione
d Aufführungsrecht

735 PERIOD COSTUME
f costume d'époque
i costume dell'epoca
d historisches Kostüm

736 PERIPETY
f péripétie
i peripezia
d Peripetie

737 PERIWIG;
PERUKE;
WIG
f perruque

i parruca
d Perücke

738 PERMANENT SET
f décor unique
i scenario unico
d ständige Dekoration

739 PERSONALITY ACTOR
f comédien qui joue son propre personnage
i attore in chiave con la parte eseguita
d Selbstdarsteller

740 PERSPECTIVE SETTING
f scène en perspective; "boite d'optique"
i scena in prospettiva
d Perspektivbühne

741 PERSPECTIVE WINGS
f décor avec coulisses en perspective
i quinte in prospettiva
d Perspektivkulissen

PERUKE see 737 PERIWIG

742 PERUQUIER; WIGMAKER
f perruquier
i parrucchiere
d Perückenmacher

743 PHLYAKES
f Phlyakes
i Fliaci
d Phlyaken

744 PHLYAX PLAYS
f Phlyakes
i Fliaci
d Phlyakenspiele

PICK OUT SOMEBODY OR SOMETHING, to, see 452 to FOCUS

PICTURE (FRAME) STAGE see 729 PEEP-SHOW

PIECE see 341 DRAMA

745 PIÈCE À CLEF
f pièce à clef
i recita a chiave
d Schlüsselstück

746 PIÈCE D'OCCASION
f pièce de circonstance
i rappresentazione di circostanza
d Gelegenheitsstück

747 PILOT LIGHT; WORKING LIGHT
f éclairage; lumière de service
i illuminazione di servizio; spia
d Arbeitslicht

748 PINCH A CALL, to
f tirer un rappel supplémentaire
i fare un'uscita in carrettell
d Vorhang schinden

PIPE BATTEN see 106 BARR

749 PIRATED EDITION
f édition illégale
i edizione illegale
d Raubausgabe

750 PIT
f parterre
i platea
d Parterre

751 PLACES PLEASE!; STAND BY!; POSITIONS PLEASE!;
f en place!
i ai vostri posti!
d auf die Plätze!

PLATFORM see 300 DAIS

752 PLATFORM STAGE
f estrade
i palco; podio
d Podiumbühne

PLAY, to, see 8 to ACT

PLAY, to, see 341 DRAMA

753 (PLAY)BILL;
PROGRAM(ME)
f programme
i programma
d Programm(heft)

754 PLAY BILL
f papillon
i cartellone; affiso teatrale
d Theaterzettel

755 PLAY DOWN TO THE
AUDIENCE, to
f s'abaisser à jouer pour le public
i abbassarsi a recitare per il pubblico; abbassarsi a recitare per un pubblico non competente
d Kinderkomödie machen

PLAYER see 733
PERFORMER

PLAY FOR AMATEURS see
41 AMATEUR THEATRICALS

PLAY FOR APPLAUSE, to,
see 630 to MILK THE
APPLAUSE

756 PLAYGOER;
THEATRE-GOER
f spectateur; amateur de théâtre
i amatore del teatro
d Theaterbesucher

757 PLAYHOUSE;
THEATRE
f théâtre
i teatro
d Theater

PLAYING AREA see 13
ACTING AREA

758 PLAY IS READY FOR
PERFORMANCE, the
f la pièce est prête
i la rappresentazione è pronta per andere in scena
d das Stück steht

759 PLAY IS SET IN LONDON, the;
the SCENE IS IN LONDON
f l'action se situe à Londres
i l'azione si svolge a Londra
d das Stück spielt in London

760 PLAY READER
f lecteur
i lettore
d Lektor

761 PLAY TO THE WOOD FAMILY,
to
f jouer devant des fauteuils vides
i recitare per le sedie
d spielen, vor leerem Haus

762 PLAY WITHIN THE PLAY
f la comédie dans la comédie
i spettacolo nello spettacolo; recita all'intero della recita
d Spiel im Spiel

763 PLAYWRIGHT;
DRAMATIST
f auteur dramatique; dramaturge
i drammaturgo; commediografo
d Bühnenautor; Dramatiker

764 PLAYWRIGHT'S THEATRE
f théâtre d'auteurs
i teatro dominato dai commediografi e drammaturghi
d Autorentheater

PLOT see 18 ACTION

765 PLOT A PLAY, to
f élaborer d'intrigue d'une pièce
i elaborare l'intreccio d'una azione; elaborare lo svolgersi d'una azione
d Handlung anlegen

766 PLOT DEVELOPMENT
f déroulement de l'intrigue
i lo svolgersi d'una azione; il procedere d'una azione
d Handlungsführung

767 POETIC DRAMA
f théâtre poétique
i recita in versi; teatro in versi
d poetisches Theater

768 POINT;
PUNCH-LINE
f piquant; sel; gag
i l'ultima battuta
d Pointe

769 POLISH, to
f fignoler
i ritoccare; perfezionare
d ausfeilen

770 PONG, to (sl.);
to WING IT (sl.)
f improviser
i improvvisare
d schwimmen (sl.)

771 PORTRAY A CHARACTER, to
f concevoir; camper un personnage
i concepire un personaggio
d eine Rolle anlegen

PORTRAYING see 12 ACTING

772 POSITION
f placement
i posizione
d Stellung

POSITIONS PLEASE! see 751 PLACES PLEASE!

773 POWDER
f poudre
i cipria
d Puder

774 PRACTICABLE (adj.)
f practicable
i praticabile
d praktikabel

775 PRECIOUS
f précieux
i prezioso; lezioso
d preziös

PRELUDE see 290 CURTAIN RAISER

PREMIERE see 437 FIRST NIGHT

PREMIER PERFORMANCE see 437 FIRST NIGHT

PERMIER PRESENTATION see 437 FIRST NIGHT

PRESENT, to, see 481 to GIV[illegible] (A PLAY)

PRESENTATION see 12 ACTI[illegible]

PRESENTATION see 732 PERFORMANCE

776 PRESENTATIONAL SETTING
f théâtre de style
i teatro di stile
d Stilbühne

777 PRESENTATION WITH STRE[illegible] ON SPECTACLE
f régie technique (des décor[illegible]
i rappresentazione spettacolare
d Bildregie

PRESTIDIGITATOR see 555 JUGGLER

778 PREVIEW PERFORMANCE; PUBLIC DRESS REHEARSAL; RÉPÉTITION GÉNÉRALE; TRY-OUT
f l'avant-première
i ante-prima
d öffentliche Generalprobe

PRINCIPAL ACTOR see 436 FIRST MAN

PRINCIPAL ACTRESS see 435 FIRST LADY

PRINCIPAL LADY see 435 FIRST LADY

PRINCIPAL MAN see 436 FIRST MAN

779 PRIVATE PERFORMANCE
f représentation privée
i rappresentazione privata
d geschlossene Vorstellung

780 PRIVATE THEATRE
f théâtre privé
i teatro privato
d Privatbühne

781 PROBABILITY; VERISIMILITUDE
f vraisemblance
i verosimiglianza
d Wahrscheinlichkeit

782 PROBLEM PLAY
f pièce à thèse
i recita a tesi
d Problemstück

PRODUCE, to, see 481 to GIVE (A PLAY)

PRODUCER see 329 DIRECTOR

783 PRODUCER'S TABLE
f pupitre du metteur en scène
i tavolo del regista
d Regiepult; Regietisch

PRODUCTION see 328 DIRECTION

784 PROFANE THEATRE; SECULAR THEATRE
f théâtre profane
i teatro profano
d weltliches Theater

785 PROFESSIONAL (ACTOR)
f comédien professionnel
i attore professionista
d Berufsschauspieler

786 PROFESSIONAL THEATRE
f théâtre professionnel
i teatro di professionisti
d Berufstheater

PROGRAM(ME) see 753 (PLAY) BILL

787 PROGRAMME; REPERTOIRE
f programme; répertoire
i programma; repertorio
d Spielplan

788 PROGRAMME SELLER
f vendeur de programmes
i venditore di programmi
d Programmverkäufer; Programmverkäuferin

789 PROJECTOR
f appareil de projection
i proiettore
d Projektionsgerät

790 PROLOGUE
f prologue
i prologo
d Prolog

PROMPT, to, see 688 to BE ON THE BOOK

791 PROMPT BOOK; PROMPT COPY; PROMPT SCRIPT; REGIEBUCH

f cahier; notes de mise en scène
i copione
d Regiebuch

792 PROMPT CORNER; PROMPTER'S BOX; PROMPTER'S CORNER (GB)
f trou du souffleur
i buca del suggeritore
d Souffleurkasten; Souffleurecke

793 PROMPTER
f souffleur
i suggeritore
d Souffleur; Einblaser

794 PROMPT SCORE
f cahier; notes de mise en scène
i quaderno di appunti del regista
d Regiepartitur

PROMPT SCRIPT see 791 PROMPT BOOK

795 PROPAGANDA PLAY
f pièce de propagande
i rappresentazione di propaganda
d Tendenzstück; Propagandastück

796 PROPERTIES; PROPS
f accessoires
i accessori
d Requisiten

797 PROPERTY MAN
f accessoiriste (du mobilier)
i trovarobe
d Requisiteur; Möbler

798 PROPERTY MASTER; PROPS (sl.)
f chef accessoiriste
i trovarobe in capo
d Requisitenmeister

799 PROPERTY MODELLER
f modeleur; constructeur d'accessoires
i trovarobe
d Kascheur

800 PROPERTY ROOM; PROPS ROOM
f loge des accessoires
i deposito accessori
d Requisitenkammer

801 PROPERTY TABLE; STAND-BY TABLE
f table des accessoires
i tavola degli accessori
d Requisitentisch

802 PROPERTY TRAP (FOR TRICKS)
f trappe à apparitions
i botola (per fare scomparire
d Reissklappe

803 PROP LIST; PROP PLOT
f liste des accessoires; conduite des accessoires
i elenco degli accessori; lista degli accessori
d Requisitenliste; Konsignation

PROPS see 796 PROPERTIES

PROPS see 798 PROPERTY MASTER

PROPS ROOM see 800 PROPERTY ROOM

804 PROSCENIUM ARCH
f l'arrondi du proscenium
i arco di proscenio
d Proszeniumbogen

805 PROSCENIUM OPENING
f ouverture de scène
i boccascena
d Bühnenöffnung

806 PROSCENIUM WING
f coulisse d'avant-scène
i quinta di proscenio
d Proszeniumkulisse

807 PROSCENIUM WINGS (GB); TORMENTORS (US)
f manteau d'Arlequin
i quinta di proscenio
d Portalseiten

808 PROSCENIUM WINGS AND BORDER (GB); TORMENTORS AND TEASERS (US)
f cadre de scène; manteau d'Arlequin
i bordo del proscenio
d Proszeniumrahmen

809 PROSE PLAY
f pièce en prose
i rappresentazione in prosa
d Prosastück

810 PROTAGONIST
f protagoniste
i protagonista
d Protagonist

811 PROTEAN ACTOR
f acteur au registre étendu
i attore versatile; attore che riesce a trasformarsi a sue piacimento
d Verwandlungsschauspieler

812 PROVINCIAL THEATRE
f théâtre de province
i teatro di provincia
d Provinztheater

813 P.S.; STAGE LEFT
f côté cour
i a sinistra del palcoscenico
d links vom Schauspieler

PUBLIC DRESS REHEARSAL see 778 PREVIEW PERFORMANCE

814 PUBLICITY
f publicité
i pubblicità
d Theaterreklame

815 PUBLIC READING (OF A DRAMA)
f lecture-spectacle
i lettura pubblica
d Leseaufführung

816 PUNCH AND JUDY SHOW
f guignol; théâtre guignol
i teatro delle marionette
d Kasperltheater

PUNCH-LINE see 768 POINT

817 PUPPET PLAYER
f marionnettiste
i marionettista
d Puppenspieler

PUPPET THEATRE see 613 MARIONETTE THEATRE

PUT ON, to, see 481 to GIVE (A PLAY)

818 QUICK CHANGE
f changement à vue
i cambiamento rapido
d Verwandlung

819 QUICK-CHANGE ROOM
f loge pour changement rapide; "guignol"
i camerino di scena
d Umkleidenische

820 RADIO PLAY
f pièce radiophonique
i commedia (o tragedia) radiofonica; rappresentazione radiofonica
d Hörspiel

RAILING see 714 PARAPET

821 RAINBOW EFFECT PROJECTOR
f projecteur pour effet d'arc-en-ciel
i proiettore per l'effetto dell'arcobaleno
d Regenbogenapparatur; Regenbogenmaschine

822 RAIN MACHINE
f machine à faire la pluie
i macchina per produrre la pioggia
d Regenmaschine

823 RAKE
f inclinaison; pente
i pendenza
d Bühnenfall

824 RAKED AUDITORIUM
f salle en gradins; salle surélevée
i sala a gradini
d überhöhter Zuschauerraum

RAMP see 445 FLOATS

RAMP see 533 INCLINED PLANE

825 RANT, to; to SHOUT
f crier; vociférer
i urlare; declamare ad alta voce
d schreien

826 RATTLE OFF, to
f bouler
i recitare troppo in fretta
d herunterrasseln

827 READING
f lecture
i lettura
d Vorlesen

READING BY THE CAST see 440 FIRST READING

READING DESK see 571 LECTERN

828 READ-THROUGH TO DISCUSS CUTS
f lecture pour décider des coupures
i lettura per decidere quali parti bisognerà sopprimere
d Strichprobe

829 REALISM
f réalisme
i realismo
d Realismus

830 RE-CAST, to
f redistribuer
i ridistribuire
d umbesetzen

831 RE-CASTING
f nouvelle distribution
i nuova ridistribuzione delle parti
d Neubesetzung

832 RECITAL; RECITATION
f recital
i recital
d Rezitation

RE-CONDITION, to, see 185 to CHANGE

833 REDERYKER SHOWS (hist.)
f chambres de rhétorique
i camere di recitazione
d Rederykerumzüge

834 RÉDUCED ADMISSION RATES
f prix réduits
i prezzi ridotti; tariffe ridotte
d ermässigte Preise

REGIEBUCH see 791 PROMPT BOOK

RÉGIME see 608 MANAGEMENT

REGULAR see 724 PATRON

835 REGULARS, the
f public régulier; les habitués
i gli abituali
d Stammpublikum

836 REHEARSAL
f répétition
i prova; ripetizione
d Probe

837 REHEARSAL AREAS; REHEARSAL ROOMS
f salles de répétitions
i sala di prova
d Probenräume

838 REHEARSAL FOR POSITIONS
f essai de mise en place
i prova per la posizione dei posti
d Setzprobe

839 REHEARSAL STAGE
f scène de répétition
i scena di prova
d Probenbühne

840 REHEARSE, to; to STUDY
f répéter; étudier
i ripetere; provare; studiare
d proben; einstudieren; (eine Rolle) lernen

841 RELIGIOUS PLAY; RITUAL PLAY
f jeu rituel
i rappresentazione religiosa
d Weihespiel; Kultspiel

842 REMOVE MAKE-UP, to
f démaquiller
i levare il trucco; togliere il trucco
d abschminken

843 RENDERING; RENDITION; REPRODUCTION
f interprétation
i interpretazione; resa
d Wiedergabe

844 RENT COSTUMES, to
f louer des costumes
i affittare costumi
d Kostüme ausleihen

REPERTOIRE see 787 PROGRAMME

845 REPERTORY (Brit.)
f répertoire
i repertorio
d Theater mit wöchentlich wechselndem Spielplan

846 REPERTORY PERFORMANC[E]
f pièce (représentation) du répertoire
i recita del repertorio
d Repertoirevorstellung

847 RÉPÉTITEUR
f répétiteur
i ripetitore
d Korrepetitor

RÉPÉTITION GÉNÉRALE see 778 PREVIEW PERFORMANC[E]

REPRESENTATIONAL STAG[E] see 528 ILLUSIONISTIC STAG[E]

REPRODUCTION see 843 RENDERING

848 RESISTANCE; RHEOSTAT
f résistance; rhéostat
i reostato; resistenza
d Widerstand

849 RE-STAGE, to
f remonter; refaire une mise en scène
i rimettere in scena
d neuinszenieren

850 RE-STUDY, to
f reprendre; remettre en chantier
i rivedere; riesaminare
d neueinstudieren

851 RETARD, to
f ralentir
i rallentare
d retardieren

REVIEW see 279 CRITICISM

REVIEWER see 278 CRITIC

852 REVIVAL
f reprise; nouvelle mise en scène
i riesumazione
d Reprise; Neuinszenierung; Wiederaufführung

853 REVOLVING PRISMS
f périactes
i scenario girevole (a forma di prisma)
d Telari

854 REVOLVING STAGE; TURNTABLE STAGE
f scène tournante; tournette
i palcoscenico girevole
d Drehbühne

855 REVUE
f pièce à grand spectacle; revue
i rivista
d Ausstattungsstück; Revue; Spektakelstück

RE-WORK, to, see 336 to DOCTOR A PLAY

RHEOSTAT see 848 RESISTANCE

856 RHETORIC
f rhéthorique
i retorica
d Rhetorik

857 "RHUBARB, RHUBARB"
f brouhaha; bruit de foule
i fare il rumore della folla
d "Rhabarber"

858 RHYTHM
f rythme
i ritmo
d Rhythmus

859 at RISE
f au lever du rideau
i all'apertura; al levarsi del sipario
d beim Aufgehen des Vorhangs

860 RISE OF THE CURTAIN
f lever du rideau
i apertura del sipario; il levarsi del sipario
d Aufgehen des Vorhangs

RITUAL PLAY see 841 RELIGIOUS PLAY

861 ROAD, THE (coll.); TOUR
f tournée (de, en province)
i tournée
d Provinztour

RÔLE see 716 PART

862 ROPE PULLEY
f moufle; poulie

i carrucola
d Seilrolle

ROSTRUM see 713 PARALLEL

863 ROUGE
f rouge
i rossetto
d Rouge

ROUND see 54 APPLAUSE

864 ROW
f rang
i fila
d Sitzreihe

865 ROYAL BOX
f loge de la Cour
i palco uffuciale; palco d'onore
d Hofloge

866 ROYALTIES
f droits d'auteur
i diritti d'autore
d Tantiemen

867 RUN-THROUGH
f enchaînement
i revisione rapida
d Durchlaufer

RUSTIC DRAMA see 726 PEASANT DRAMA

SAFETY CURTAIN see 68 ASBESTOS CURTAIN

868 SAFETY PRECAUTIONS INSPECTOR
f Inspecteur des services de sécurité
i Ispettore dei servizi di sicurezza
d Bühneninspektor

869 SALARY
f cachet
i paga; retribuzione
d Gage

870 SANDBAG
f sac de sable
i sacchetto di sabbia
d Sandsack

871 SATIRE
f satire
i satira
d Satire

872 SATYR PLAY
f drame satyrique
i dramma satirico
d Satyrspiel

873 SAVE A SCENE, to
f sauver une scène
i salvare una scena
d eine Szene retten

874 SCAFFOLDING
f échafaudage
i impalcatura
d Gerüst

SCAFFOLD STAGE see 129 BOOTH STAGE

875 SCALPER (US); TOUT (GB)
f revendeur de billets
i rivenditore di biglietti
d Agioteur

876 SCAN, to
f scander
i scandire
d skandieren

877 SCENE
f scène
i scena
d Szene

878 SCENE; STAGE
f scène; théâtre
i scena
d Bühne

879 SCENE BASED ON FLIGHTS OF STAIRS
f scène à plans étagés
i scena a piani sovrapposti
d Treppenbühne

880 SCENE-BUILDING; SKENE
f skene (scène antique)
i scena (del teatro antico)
d Skene

881 SCENE CHANGE
f changement de scène
i cambiamento di scena
d Szenenwechsel

882 SCENE DESIGN
f projet; esquisse de décor
i modellino (della scena); plastico
d Bühnenbildentwurf

883 SCENE DESIGNER; SCENIC DESIGNER; SET DESIGNER; STAGE DECORATOR
f décorateur
i decoratore
d Bühnenbildner; Dekorateur

884 SCENE DIRECTION
f indication scénique
i indicazione di scena
d Szenenanweisung

SCENE IS SET IN LONDON, THE see 759 THE PLAY IS SET IN LONDON

SCENE OF ACTION see 591 LOCALE

885 SCENE PAINTER;
SCENIC ARTIST
f peintre de décor; décorateur
i decoratore
d Theatermaler

886 SCENE REHEARSAL;
TECHNICAL REHEARSAL
f répétition technique (décors)
i prova delle scene
d Dekorationsprobe

SCENERY see 309 DÉCOR

887 SCENERY STORE
f magasin de décors
i deposito delle scene
d Dekorationsmagazin

888 SCENE SHIFTER
f machiniste
i macchinista
d Kulissenschieber

889 SCENE SKETCH
f esquisse de décor
i disegno della scena; schizzo
d Dekorationsskizze

890 SCENIC ARRANGEMENT
f arrangement scénique
i adattamento scenico
d Bühnengestaltung

SCENIC ARTIST see 885 SCENE PAINTER

891 SCENIC CONTRACTOR
f scénographe
i scenografo
d Bühnenarchitekt

892 SCENIC DESIGN;
STAGE DESIGN;
STAGE PICTURE
f décor
i decorazione della scena
d Bühnenbild; Bild

SCENIC DESIGNER see 883 SCENE DESIGNER

893 SCENIC MAGNIFICENCE;
SUMPTUOUS DECOR
f décor; décoration (costumes, accessoires compris); décor somptueux
i suntuosità della scena; scena suntuosa
d Ausstattung

894 SCENIC MODEL
f maquette de la scène
i plastico; modellino (della scena)
d Maquette

895 SCENIC REHEARSAL
f répétition technique générale
i prova tecnica
d technische Hauptprobe

SCHEDULE see 164 CALL LIST

896 SCHOOL DRAMA
f pièce pour collège
i recita per collegio
d Schuldrama

SCHOOL OF ACTING see 345 DRAMATIC SCHOOL

SCHOOL OF DRAMATIC ART see 345 DRAMATIC SCHOOL

897 SCHOOL PERFORMANCE
f représentation scolaire
i rappresentazione scolastica
d Schülervorstellung

898 SCHOOL THEATRE
f théâtre scolaire
i teatro scolastico
d Schultheater

899 SCREEN
f paravent; écran
i schermo; paravento
d Paravent

900 SCRIM
f gaze; canevas léger; tulle
i canapa finissima
d Rupfen; Gaze

901 SCRIPT
f manuscrit
i copione
d Manuskript

SCRIPT see 575 LIBRETTO

SCRIPT READING see 440 FIRST READING

902 SEASON
f saison théâtrale
i stagione teatrale
d Saison; Spielzeit

903 SEASON TICKET; SUBSCRIPTION (TICKET)
f abonnement
i abbonamento
d Abonnement

904 SEAT
f place
i posto
d Platz; Sitz

905 SEATING CAPACITY
f capacité de la salle; nombre de places
i capacità della sala; numero dei posti; disponibilità della sala; capienza della sala
d Fassungsvermögen; Sitzanzahl

906 SEATING PLAN; SHEET
f plan de location
i pianta dei posti
d Sitzplan

907 SECONDARY LIGHTING SYSTEM
f éclairage de secours
i illuminazione di sicurezza
d Notbeleuchtung

SECULAR THEATRE see 784 PROFANE THEATRE

SECURE, to, see 416 to FASTEN

SENTIMENTAL COMEDY see 563 LACHRYMOSE COMEDY

SENTIMENTAL DRAMA see 564 LACHRYMOSE DRAMA

908 SEQUENCE
f succession des tableaux
i sequenza
d Bildfolge

909 SET (A SCENE), to
f monter; planter (un décor)
i montare una scena
d aufbauen

SET DESIGNER see 883 SCENE DESIGNER

910 SET OF COUNTERWEIGHT LINES
f équipe à contrepoinds
i insieme dei contrappesi
d Gegengewichtszug

911 SET OF LINES
f équipes du lointain
i stangone del fondale
d Prospektzug

912 SET PIECE
f décor mobile; ferme
i scena montata su telaio
d Versatzstück

913 SETTING MADE OF BLOCKS
f scène architecturée
i costruzioni
d Blockbühne

SETTINGS see 309 DÉCOR

SHADE see 676 NUANCE

914 SHADOW PLAY
f théâtre d'ombre
i teatro d'ombre
d Schattenspiel

915 SHARING TERMS, to BE PAID ON
f être payé au pourcentage
i esser pagato al tanto per cento; essere pagato a percentuale
d auf Teilung spielen

SHEET see 906 SEATING PLAN

916 SHIFT, to
f modifier (le décor)
i cambiare
d umräumen

"SHOP" see 376 ENGAGEMENT

SHOUT, to, see 825 to RANT

SHOW see 732 PERFORMANCE

917 SHOW;
SPECTACLE
f show
i spettacolo; show
d Schaustück

918 SHOW BUSINESS
f théâtre; département du théâtre
i il mondo del teatro
d Theaterwesen

919 SHOW BUSINESS;
THEATRE ENTERPRISE
THE TRADE
f entreprise théâtrale
i impresa teatrale
d Theaterbetrieb

920 SHROVETIDE PLAY
f pièce de Mardi Gras
i rappresentazione del martedì grasso
d Fastnachtsspiel

921 SHUTTERS;
VENETIAN BLINDS
f jalousies
i persiane; veneziane
d Jalousien

922 SIDE ACTION;
SUB-PLOT
f intrigue secondaire
i intreccio secondario; azione secondaria
d Nebenhandlung

923 SIDE STAGE
f scène latérale
i scena laterale
d Seitenbühne

924 SIGHT LINES
f lignes de visibilité
i linee di visibilità
d Sehlinien; Sichtlinien

925 SILHOUETTE SETTING
f décor en silhouettes; théâtre d'ombres
i scena in silhouette
d Silhouettenbühne

SIMULTANEOUS SET;
SIMULTANEOUS SETTING
see 311 DÉCOR SIMULTANÉ

SIMULTANEOUS STAGE see 654 MULTIPLE STAGE

926 SINGER
f chanteur; chanteuse
i cantante
d Sänger; Sängerin

SINKING STAGE see 368 ELEVATOR STAGE

927 SIT ON ONE'S HANDS, to (audience)
f applaudir du bout des doigts
i non applaudire; rifiutarsi di applaudire
d auf den Händen sitzen

928 SITUATION HUMOUR
f comique de situation
i spirito di situazione
d Situationskomik

929 SIZE PAINT
f vernis; colle à barbe
i appretto; colla speciale
d Leimfarbe

930 SKELETON SET
f décor sommaire
i scena ridotta
d angedeutete Dekoration

SKENE see 880 SCENE-BUILDING

931 SKETCH;
SKIT
f sketch; saynête
i sketch
d Sketch

SKY DOME see 297 CYCLORAMA DOME

SLAPSTICK COMEDY see 561 KNOCK-ABOUT COMEDY

SLATE, to, see 273 to CRAB

932 SLIDING STAGE
f scène coulissante
i palcoscenico scorrevole
d Schiebebühne

933 SLIP OF THE TONGUE
f lapsus
i lapsus
d Versprechen

934 SLOAT
f cassette
i gabbia
d Kassette

935 SLOAT CUT FLAP
f couvercle de cassette
i apertura per sollevamento delle scene
d Kassettenklappe

936 SLOPE
f surélévation
i pendenza
d Uberhöhung

937 SMALL CHARACTER PART;
SUPPORTING ROLE;
UTILITY ROLE
f utilité
i parte secondaria
d Chargenrolle

SMALL PART see 116 BIT

938 SMALL PART ACTOR
f comédien secondaire (qui joue les utilités)
i attore secondario
d Nebendarsteller; Chargendarsteller

939 SMALL PART MAN
f comédien secondaire (qui joue les utilités)
i attore secondario
d Nebendarsteller; Chargendarsteller

940 SMALL PART WOMAN
f comédienne secondaire (qui joue les utilités)
i attrice secondaria
d Nebendarstellerin; Chargendarstellerin

941 SMOKE OUTLET;
SMOKE LOUVRE
f cheminée d'appel
i uscita del fumo
d Rauchklappe

942 SMOKING ROOM
f fumoir
i salotto per fumatori
d Rauchsalon

SOB-DRAMA see 564 LACHRYMOSE DRAMA

943 SOCIAL DRAMA
f drame social
i dramma sociale
d Sozialdrama

SOLD OUT see 523 "HOUSE FULL"

SOLILOQUY see 645 MONOLOGUE

944 SOLUTION
f solution
i soluzione
d Lösung

945 SONG
f chanson
i canzone
d Couplet

SOOT-AND-WHITEWASH CHARACTERIZATION see 117 BLACK-AND-WHITE PORTRAITURE

946 SOUBRETTE
f soubrette
i canzonettista; soubrette
d Soubrette

947 SOUND-ABSORBING
f amortisseur (de son)
i atutizzatore del suono
d schallschluckend

948 SOUND EFFECTS
f effets sonores
i effetti sonori
d akustische Effekte

SOUND MIXING TABLE see 707 PANATROPE

949 SOUND TECHNIQUE
f technique du son
i tecnica del suono
d Tontechnik

950 SOUSRÉGISSEUR;
ASSISTANT STAGE MANAGER
f sans equiv. (metteur en scène chargé d'assister à la représentation)
i aiuto del direttore tecnico delle scene
d Abendregisseur

SOUSRÉGISSEUR see 72 ASSISTANT STAGE MANAGER

951 SPEAK IN A LOW VOICE, to
f parler à voix basse
i parlare a voce bassa; parlare sottovoce
d leise sprechen

SPEAKING PART see 717 PART IN A NON-MUSICAL PLAY

952 SPEAKING VOICE
f voix parlée
i dizione
d Sprechstimme

953 SPEAK UP!
f plus fort
i più forte!
d lauter sprechen!

SPECIALIST see 193 CHARACTER MAN

SPECTACLE see 917 SHOW

954 SPECTATOR
f spectateur
i spettatore
d Zuschauer

955 SPIRIT GUM; MASTIC
f mastic
i mastice
d Mastix

956 SPIRITUAL ESSENCE
f contenu spirituel
i contenuto spirituale
d geistiger Gehalt

SPOIL AN EFFECT, to, see 639 to MISS A POINT

SPONSOR see 44 ANGEL

SPOT, to, see 452 to FOCUS

957 SPOTLIGHT
f projecteur à grande concentration
i proiettore; riflettore
d Punktscheinwerfer

958 SPOTLIGHTS AND FLOODLIGHTS
f projecteurs
i riflettori; proiettori
d Scheinwerfer

959 SPRINKLER SYSTEM
f système sprinkler; rideau d'eau
i impianto antincendio; sistema antincendio
d Regenanlage; Sprinkleranlage

S.R.O. see 994 STANDING ROOM ONLY

STAGE see 878 SCENE

STAGE, to, see 481 to GIVE (A PLAY)

960 STAGE BOARDS
f les planches
i palcoscenico
d Bühnenbretter

961 STAGE BOX
f loge d'avant-scène
i palco di proscenio
d Proszeniumloge

962 STAGE BUILDING
f cage de scène
i vano della scena
d Bühnenhaus

963 STAGE CLOTH
f tapis de scène
i tappeto
d Bühnenteppich

964 STAGECRAFT
f technique de la scénographie
i scenotecnica
d Bühnenkunde

STAGE CREW see 499 GRIP HAND

STAGE DECORATOR see 883 SCENE DESIGNER

STAGE DESIGN see 892 SCENIC DESIGN

965 STAGE DIRECTIONS
f indications de mise en scène
i didascalia
d Regieanweisungen

966 STAGE DIRECTOR'S OFFICE
f bureau du metteur en scène
i ufficio del regista
d Regiekanzlei

967 STAGE DOOR
f entrée des artistes; porte de scène

i entrata degli artisti; entrata della scena
d Bühneneingang; Bühnentür

968 STAGE-DOOR KEEPER
f gardien; portier
i portiere; guardiano
d Bühnenportier

969 STAGE FLOOR
f plateau; plancher de scène
i pavimento del palcoscenico
d Bühnenboden

STAGE FRIGHT see 669 NERVES

STAGE HAND see 499 GRIP HAND

970 STAGE HOG
f cabotin
i istrione; attore che ingombra il centro della scena a discapito di un altro
d Kulissenreisser

STAGE LEFT see 813 P.S.

971 STAGE LEVELS
f niveaux de scène; niveaux de jeu
i livelli di scena
d Spielebenen

972 STAGE MACHINERY
f machinerie
i attrezzatura
d Bühnenmaschinerie

973 STAGE MACHINERY (AT STAGE LEVEL)
f machinerie de plateau
i attrezzatura del palcoscenico
d Bodenmaschinerie

974 STAGE MACHINIST
f machiniste en chef
i macchinista
d Theatermeister

STAGEMANAGE, to, see 327 to DIRECT

975 STAGE MANAGER; SM
f régisseur de plateau
i regista
d Inspizient

STAGE MANAGER see 330 DIRECTOR

976 STAGE MANAGER'S DESK
f pupitre de régie
i tavolo del regista
d Inspizientenpult

977 STAGE NAME
f pseudonyme
i nome d'arte; pseudonimo
d Künstlername

STAGE PICTURE see 892 SCENIC DESIGN

978 STAGE PLAY
f pièce de théâtre
i commedia (o tragedia) teatrale; rappresentazione teatrale
d Bühnenstück

979 STAGE REHEARSAL
f répétition sur scène
i prova sulla scena
d Bühnenprobe

980 STAGE RIGHT; O.P.
f côté jardin
i a destra del palcoscenico
d rechts vom Schauspieler

STAGE RIGHTS see 734 PERFORMING RIGHTS

981 STAGE SCREW
f queue de cochon
i vite di fissaggio per teatro
d Bohrer

STAGE SET see 309 DÉCOR

982 STAGE SLANG
f jargon de théâtre; argot de coulisses
i gergo di teatro; gergo della scena; linguaggio del teatro
d Theaterjargon

983 STAGE-STRUCK
f fou de théâtre
i appasionato di teatro
d theatertoll

984 STAGE TECHNICIAN
f technicien
i tecnico
d Bühnentechniker

985 STAGE TECHNIQUE
f technique de la scène
i tecnica della scena
d Bühnentechnik

986 STAGE TOWER
f tourelle; cage de scène
i torrette
d Bühnenturm

STAGE VERSION see 14 ACTING EDITION

987 STAGE WAIT
f blanc; trou
i vuoto; silenzio
d Loch (sl.)

988 STAGEY; THEATRICAL
f théâtral; scénique
i teatrale; istrionico
d theatralisch

STAGIONE PERFORMANCE see 503 GUEST PERFORMANCE

989 STALLS
f fauteuils d'orchestre
i poltrone d'orchestra
d Parkett

990 STAND
f tribune
i tribuna
d Tribüne

991 STANDBY; STOPGAP
f bouche trou
i riempi buchi
d Lückenbüsser

STAND BY!; see 751 PLACES PLEASE!

STAND-BY TABLE see 801 PROPERTY TABLE

992 STANDEE (coll.)
f spectateur debout
i uditore in piedi
d Stehplatzbesucher

993 STANDING ROOM
f place debout
i posto in piedi
d Stehplatz

994 STANDING ROOM ONLY; S.R.O.
f Il n'y a plus de places assises
i soltanto posti in piedi
d nur noch Stehplätze

995 STANZA; STROPHE
f strophe
i strofa; stanza
d Strophe

STAR see 335 DIVA

STATE THEATRE see 419 FEDERAL THEATRE

STEAL THE SHOW, to, see 247 to COME TO THE FRONT

STEELY VOICE see 626 METALLIC VOICE

STICK, to, see 99 to BALLOON

996 STICK OF GREASE PAINT
f bâton de fard
i bastoncino per il trucco
d Schminkstift

STOCK see 238 COLLECTION

997 STOCK CHARACTERS
f personnages du répertoire
i personaggi del repertorio
d stehende Typen

998 STOCK OF SCENERY
f magasin de décors
i scorta di scenari
d Kulissenfundus

STOOGE see 420 FEED

STOPGAP see 991 STANDBY

STORAGE ROOMS see 316 DEPOT

STORAGE SPACE see 316 DEPOT

999 STORM AND STRESS
f "Sturm und Drang"
i Sturm und Drang
d Sturm und Drang

STORY see 18 ACTION

1000 STRAIGHT CEILING PIECE
f plafond simple
i soffitto semplice
d einfacher Plafond

STRAIGHT PART see 717 PART IN A NON-MUSICAL PLAY

STRAIGHT PLAY see 673 NON-MUSICAL DRAMA

1001 STRAWHAT THEATRE (coll.) SUMMER THEATRE
f théâtre d'été
i teatro estivo; teatro d'estate
d Sommertheater

1002 STRIKE, to (scenery)
f déblayer (scène)
i sgombrare la scena
d abbauen

STRING PUPPET THEATRE see 613 MARIONETTE THEATRE

STROLLING PLAYERS see 104 BARNSTORMERS

STROPHE see 995 STANZA

1003 STUDENT ACTOR
f apprenti-comédien
i allievo attore
d Eleve

1004 STUDIO THEATRE
f théâtre d'essai
i teatro sperimentale; teatro di prova
d Ateliertheater; Studiotheater

STUDY, to, see 840 to REHEARSE

1005 STUDY OF MOVEMENT
f mise en place
i studio del movimiento
d Bewegungsregie

1006 STYLIZE, to
f styliser
i stilizzare
d stilisieren

SUB-PLOT see 922 SIDE ACTION

SUBSCRIPTION (TICKET) see 903 SEASON TICKET

1007 SUBSIDIZED THEATRE
f théâtre subventionné
i teatro sovvenzionato
d subventioniertes Theater

SUCCESS see 521 HIT

1008 SUCCES D'ESTIME
f succès d'estime
i successo di stima
d Achtungserfolg

SUMMER THEATRE see 1001 STRAWHAT THEATRE

SUMPTUOUS DECOR see 893 SCENIC MAGNIFICENCE

1009 SUPERFICIAL; SURFACE-DRAWN
f superficiel
i superficiale
d vordergründig

SUPERNUMERARIES, SUPERS see 402 EXTRAS

SUPER(NUMERARY) see 401 EXTRA

1010 SUPPORTING ACTOR
f second rôle; faire-valoir
i attore di secondo piano
d Nebendarsteller

1011 SUPPORTING CAST
f les seconds rôles; la troupe, qui seconde les premiers rôles
i l'insieme dei personaggi di secondo piano
d Nebendarsteller

SUPPORTING ROLE see 937 SMALL CHARACTER PART

SURFACE-DRAWN see 1009 SUPERFICIAL

1012 SWAG BORDER
f lambrequin
i fregio
d Schmuckleiste

1013 SWITCH BOARD
f tableau; tableau de commande
i quadro elettrico
d Schaltbrett

1014 SYMBOLIST
f symboliste
i simbolista
d symbolistisch

1015 SYNTHETIC DRAMA
f théâtre synthétique; théâtre total
i teatro sintetico
d synthetisches Drama

1016 TAB CURTAIN
- f rideau à l'italienne
- i sipario all'italiana
- d Raffvorhang; Wagnergardine

1017 TABLEAU
- f tableau
- i quadro
- d Tableau

1018 TABLEAU VIVANT
- f tableau vivant
- i quadro animato
- d lebendes Bild

1019 TAKE A CURTAIN CALL, to
- f saluer
- i presentarsi alla ribalta
- d sich verbeugen

TAKINGS see 139 BOX-OFFICE RECEIPTS

1020 TALENT; NATURAL GIFT
- f talent
- i talento
- d Begabung

1021 TALENT SCOUT
- f sans equiv. (celui qui cherche des talents)
- i scopritore di talenti
- d Talentsucher

1022 TAPE CECORDER
- f magnétophone
- i magnetofono; registratore
- d Magnetophon; Tonbandgerät

TAWDRY see 473 GARISH

TEAM PLAYING see 379 ENSEMBLE PLAYING

TEAR-JERKER see 564 LACHRYMOSE DRAMA

TEAR TO PIECES, to, see 273 to CRAB

1023 TECHNICAL DIRECTOR
- f directeur technique
- i direttore tecnico
- d technischer Leiter

TECHNICAL REHEARSAL see 886 SCENE REHEARSAL

1024 TELEVISION PLAY; TV PLAY
- f pièce pour la télévision
- i recita per la televisione
- d Fernsehstück

TENANT see 572 LESSEE

1025 TENDENCY PLAY; THESIS PLAY
- f pièce à thèse
- i rappresentazione a tesi
- d Tendenzstück

1026 TENNIS-COURT (hist.)
- f Jeu de Paume
- i Giuoco della Pallacorda
- d Ballhaus

1027 TERENCE STAGE
- f la scène de Térence
- i la scena di Terenzio
- d Terenzbühne

1028 TERROR AND PITY
- f la crainte et la pitié
- i il terrore e la pietà
- d Furcht und Mitleid

1029 TETRALOGY
- f tétralogie
- i tetralogia
- d Tetralogie

TEXT see 575 LIBRETTO

THEATRE see 757 PLAYHOUSE

1030 THEATRE CRAFT; THEATRICAL SCIENCE

f science du théâtre (université)
i tecnica teatrale
d Theaterwissenschaft

THEATRE ENTERPRISE see 919 SHOW BUSINESS

THEATRE-GOER see 756 PLAYGOER

THEATRE-IN-THE-ROUND see 61 ARENA STAGE

THEATRE SCHOOL see 345 DRAMATIC SCHOOL

1031 THEATRE STAFF
f personnel de scène
i personale del teatro
d Bühnepersonal

THEATRICAL see 988 STAGEY

THEATRICALS see 732 PERFORMANCE

THEATRICAL SCIENCE see 1030 THEATRE CRAFT

THESIS PLAY see 1025 TENDENCY PLAY

1032 THICKNESS PIECE
f épaisseur
i spessore
d Dickung

1033 THREE-DIMENSIONAL SCENERY
f décor volume modelé
i scena a tre dimensioni
d kaschierte Szenerie

1034 THREE UNITIES, the (time, action, place)
f les trois unités
i le tre unità
d die drei Einheiten

1035 THRILLER
f pièce policière
i recita poliziesca; spettacolo giallo
d Kriminalstück

1036 THROAT, to HAVE A FROG IN ONE'S
f gorge, avoir un chat dans la
i arrocchire; affiochire
d Hals, einem Frosch im - haben

1037 THROW LINE
f guinde
i corda per congiugere
d Schlagschnur; Wurfleine

1038 THROW-LINE CLEAT
f sauterelle (de guinde)
i gancio per legare; viti per legare
d Einwurfhaken

1039 THUNDER BALLS; THUNDER STONES
f boulets pour effets de tonnerre
i palle per effetto sonore di tuono
d Nachhallbälle

1040 THUNDER CART; THUNDER GALLERY
f machine à faire le tonnerre
i macchina per (l'effetto del) tuono
d Donnermaschine

1041 THUNDER CRASH
f coup de tonnerre
i colpo di tuono
d Einschlag

1042 THUNDER DRUM
f tambour à faire le tonnerre
i tamburo per (l'effetto del) tuono
d Donnerpauke

THUNDER GALLERY see 1040 THUNDER CART

1043 THUNDER RUN
f machine à faire le tonnerre
i macchina per (produrre il) tuono
d Fallkasten

1044 THUNDER SHEET
f tôle (bruitage de tonnerre)
i lamiera (per effetto del) tuono
d Donnerblech

THUNDER STONES see 1039 THUNDER BALLS

TICKET see 721 PASTEBOARD

1045 TICKETS AT THE BOX OFFICE
f billets à la caisse
i i biglietti si possono ritirare alla cassa!
d Karten an der Abendkasse

TIER see 216 CIRCLE

1046 TIGHTS
f collant; maillot
i calzamaglia
d Trikot

1047 TIGHT STRUCTURE
f structure dramatique serrée; construction dramatique serrée
i costruzione serrata
d straffe Struktur

1048 TIME, to (the play)
f minuter
i prendere il tempo
d abstoppen

TIME-TABLE see 164 CALL LIST

1049 TIRADE
f tirade
i tirata
d Tirade

TITLE ROLE see 663 NAME PART

1050 TOP BATTEN
f perche du dessus
i assicella superiore; traversa superiore
d Oberlatte

1051 TOPICAL DRAMA
f pièce d'actualité
i recita d'attualità
d Zeitstück

1052 TORCH
f flambeau; torche
i fiaccola
d Fackel

TORMENTORS see 807 PROSCENIUM WINGS

TORMENTORS AND TEASERS see 808 PROSCENIUM WINGS AND BORDER

TORMENTOR SPOT see 731 PERCH SPOT

1053 TOTAL THEATRE
f théâtre total
i teatro totale
d Totaltheater

1054 TOUPÉE
f toupet
i tuppè
d Toupet

TOUR see 861 THE ROAD

TOURING COMPANY see 104 BARNSTORMERS

1055 TOUR THE PROVINCES, to
f présenter un spectacle sans intérêt
i fare una tournée in provincia
d auf die Dörfer gehen

TOUT see 875 SCALPER

TRACK see 504 GUIDE

TRADE, the, see 919 SHOW BUSINESS

1056 TRAGEDIAN; TRAGIC ACTOR
f tragédien
i tragediante; attore tragico
d Tragöde

1057 TRAGEDIENNE; TRAGIC ACTRESS
f tragédienne
i tragediante; attrice tragica
d Tragödin

1058 TRAGEDY
f tragédie
i tragedia
d Tragödie; Trauerspiel

1059 TRAGEDY OF FATE
f tragédie du Destin
i tragedia del Destino
d Schicksalstragödie

TRAGIC ACTOR see 1056 TRAGEDIAN

TRAGIC ACTRESS see 1057 TRAGEDIENNE

1060 TRAGI-COMEDY
f tragi-comédie
i tragi-commedia
d Tragikomödie

1061 TRAINING
f formation; métier
i preparazione; formazione; esercizio
d Ausbildung

1062 TRANSPARENCY LINEN
f voile transparent (pour décor par transparence)
i velo trasparente
d Schirting

1063 TRAP DOOR
f trappe
i botola
d Versenkung

TRAPPINGS see 309 DÉCOR

1064 TRASH
f le clinquant
i rappresentazione di cattivo gusto
d Kitsch

TRASHY see 473 GARISH

1065 TRAVESTY
f travesti
i parodia; travestimento (comico)
d Travestie

TREADMILL see 263 CONVEYOR BELT

TREASURY OF DRAMA see 342 THE DRAMA

1066 TRICK-LINE
f ficelle
i fune; tiri
d Trick

1067 TRILOGY
f trilogie
i trilogia
d Trilogie

TROOP see 101 BAND

TROUPE see 101 BAND

1068 TROWEL, to LAY IT ON WITH A
f exagérer; charger; insister lourdement
i esagerare; insistere molto; adulare grossolanamente
d dick auftragen

TRY-OUT see 778 PREVIEW PERFORMANCE

1069 TUMBLER;
BOTTOM BATTEN
f polichinelle
i pertica inferiore; acrobata
d Unterlatte

1070 TURN
f numéro; attraction
i numero; attrazione
d Programmnummer; Nummer (Varieté)

TURNTABLE STAGE see 854 REVOLVING STAGE

1071 TV PLAY;
TELEVISION PLAY
f pièce pour la télévision
i recita per la televisione
d Fernsehstück

TV PLAY see 1024 TELEVISION PLAY

TWO-HANDKERCHIEF DRAMA see 564 LACHRYMOSE DRAMA

TWO LINES AND A SPIT see 116 BIT

TYPE see 189 CHARACTER CATEGORY

1072 TYPE OF DRAMA
f genre dramatique
i genere drammatico di rappresentazione
d Dramengattung

1073 UNDER MACHINERY
f machinerie des dessous
i attrezzi di sottopalco; macchinari di sottopalco
d Untermaschinerie

1074 UNDERPLAY, to
f jouer en dessous (du ton)
i recitare in maniera controllata
d unterspielen

1075 UNDERSTAGE
f les dessous
i sottopalco
d Unterbühne

UNDERSTUDY see 374 EMERGENCY UNDERSTUDY

UNDERSTUDY, to, see 489 to GO ON FOR SOMEBODY

1076 UNIFIED WORK OF ART
f oeuvre d'art totale; synthèse artistique
i sintesi artistica
d Gesamtkunstwerk

1077 UNITY
f unité
i unità
d Einheit

UNIVERSITY THEATRE see 165 CAMPUS THEATRE

1078 UNMADE-UP
f sans maquillage
i senza trucco
d ungeschminkt

UPPER BALCONY see 471 GALLERY

1079 UPPER CIRCLE
f première galerie
i prima galleria
d zweiter Rang

1080 UNREWARDING PART
f rôle ingrat
i parte ingrata
d undankbare Rolle

1081 UP-STAGE
f lointain
i fondale
d hinten

1082 USHER; USHERETTE
f placeur; ouvreuse
i maschera
d Platzanweiser; Platzanweiserin; Billeteur; Billeteuse

UTILITY ROLE see 937 SMALL CHARACTER PART

VARIETY see 659 MUSIC HALL

1083 VAUDEVILLE
f vaudeville
i vaudeville
d Vaudeville

VENETIAN BLINDS see 921 SHUTTERS

1084 VENTILATION
f ventilation
i ventilazione
d Ventilation

1085 VENTRILOQUIST
f ventriloque
i ventriloquo
d Bauchredner

VERISIMILITUDE see 781 PROBABILITY

1086 VERSE DRAMA
f pièce en vers
i dramma in versi
d Versdrama

1087 VERSION
f version
i versione
d Fassung

VET A PLAY, to, see 336 to DOCTOR A PLAY

1088 VIEW;
VISIBILITY
f visibilité
i visibilità
d Sicht

1089 VILLAIN
f coquin; fripon; traître
i antagonista; traditore
d Bösewicht; Schurke

1090 VIRTUOSO
f virtuose
i virtuoso
d Virtuose

VISIBILITY see 1088 VIEW

1091 VISITING DIRECTOR;
VISITING PRODUCER
f metteur en scène engagé au spectacle
i regista invitato
d Gastregisseur

VOICE TECHNIQUE see 370 ELOCUTION

WAGON see 124 BOAT TRUCK

1092 WAGON STAGE
f scène à plateaux coulissants
i palcoscenico scorrevole
d Wagenbühne

1093 WALK ON, to
f figurer
i fare da comparsa
d statieren

1094 WARDROBE
f atelier de costumes
i laboratorio della costumista
d Kostümwerkstatt

WARDROBE see 200 CHECK ROOM

1095 WARDROBE DIRECTOR
f chef costumier
i capo costumista
d Gewandmeister

1096 WARDROBE MASTER; WARDROBE MISTRESS
f costumier; costumière
i costumista
d Garderobemeister(in)

1097 WARM AUDIENCE
f public chaleureux; bon public
i pubblico entusiasta
d mitgehendes Publikum

1098 WARNING BELL
f sonnerie
i segnale
d Glockenzeichen

1099 WEEKLY RAPPORT
f chronique théâtrale
i cronaca teatrale settimanale
d Theaterbericht

1100 WHITE LEAD
f céruse
i cerussa
d Bleiweiss

WIG see 737 PERIWIG

WIGMAKER see 742 PERUQUIER

1101 WIND MACHINE
f machine à faire le vent
i macchina a vento; macchina per creare l'effetto del vento
d Windmaschine

1102 WING
f coulisse
i quinta
d Kulisse

1103 WING-AND-BORDER STAGE
f scène à coulisses
i scena a quinte
d Kulissenbühne

1104 WING CARRIAGE
f chariot
i attrezzatura per le quinte
d Kulissenwagen

1105 WING-CARRIAGE (Continental theatre)
f chariot de dessous; système à costières
i carretto per le quinte
d Freifahrt

WING IT, to, see 770 to PONG

WING IT, to, see 99 to BALLOON

1106 WITH THE CURTAIN UP
f en cours de représentation; rideau levé
i a scena aperta
d auf offener Szene

1107 WORD PERFECT, the ACTOR IS
- f le texte est su
- i l'attore conosce perfettamente il testo
- d der Text sitzt

WORD PERFECT, to be see 573 to be LETTER PERFECT

1108 WORD REHEARSAL
- f répétition à l'italienne
- i prova del testo
- d Durchsprechprobe

1109 WORD SCENERY
- f décor évoqué verbalement
- i scenario evocato verbalmente
- d gesprochene Dekoration

WORKING LIGHT see 747 PILOT LIGHT

1110 WORKROOM DIRECTOR
- f chef d'atelier
- i direttore di studio
- d Werkstättenmeister

1111 WORKSHOP
- f atelier
- i studio
- d Werkstatt; Werkstätte

1112 WORKSHOP PRODUCTION
- f représentation d'un théâtre d'essai
- i produzione del teatro di prova
- d Studioaufführung

1113 WORLD PREMIERE
- f création mondiale
- i prima rappresentazione mondiale; prima mondiale
- d Welturaufführung

1114 WRITE A PART FOR AN ACTOR, to
- f écrire un rôle pour un acteur
- i scrivere appositamente una parte per un attore
- d auf den Leib schreiben (jemand eine Rolle)

1115 WRONG CUE
- f (entrer à la, envoyer la) mauvaise réplique
- i battuta sbagliata
- d falscher Einsatz

INDEXES

FRANÇAIS

ITALIANO

DEUTSCH